COUNTING HER H

Riverbend, Texas Heat 3

Marla Monroe

MENAGE EVERLASTING

Siren Publishing, Inc.
www.SirenPublishing.com

A SIREN PUBLISHING BOOK
IMPRINT: Ménage Everlasting

COUNTING HER BLESSINGS
Copyright © 2012 by Marla Monroe

ISBN: 978-1-62241-760-5

First Printing: October 2012

Cover design by Les Byerley
All art and logo copyright © 2012 by Siren Publishing, Inc.

Printed in the U.S.A.

PUBLISHER
Siren Publishing, Inc.
www.SirenPublishing.com

COUNTING HER BLESSINGS

Riverbend, Texas Heat 3

MARLA MONROE
Copyright © 2012

Chapter One

Caitlyn drove past the sign that said *Welcome to Riverbend, Texas, population 345,* and continued into town. It was close to 9:00 p.m., and she was about done in. Her brother promised to meet her at the diner to show her how to get out to his house. Her navigation package didn't include newly built roads. She pulled into the diner right where he said it would be and climbed out of her Pathfinder. Her legs were stiff from the long drive from Jackson, Mississippi. He would have a fit when he found out she had left her house at eight the night before and driven straight through. Twenty-four hours without stopping except for gas and bathroom breaks took a toll on a person.

She walked into the diner, dead on her feet, and found a booth where she could watch for his truck. She pulled out her cell phone and dialed his number. It went to voice mail. She left a message and had just punched off when the waitress, a sweet-looking young woman, walked up to take her order.

"What can I get for you?"

"Diet Coke and a grilled cheese sandwich, if you don't mind."

"Want fries with it?"

"No, thanks."

The waitress smiled and walked off to fill her drink order. She couldn't see much of the place in the dark, but Brian seemed real happy with the town. Considering his predilection for a ménage relationship, she supposed he was lucky to have found somewhere that would accept him and his *family*. Not many places would.

She sighed and ran a hand through her hair. She needed a bed and soon. She didn't think she could stay awake much longer.

"Here's your drink, ma'am. You passing through?"

"Oh, um, thanks. No. I'm visiting my brother. He's supposed to meet me here."

"Who's your brother?"

"Brian Southworth."

"Sure, I know him. He and Tish and Andy are getting married next week. Welcome to Riverbend."

"Thanks."

"Your grilled cheese will be out in just a few minutes."

By the time she had finished her grilled cheese, she was seriously fighting sleep. She tried calling her brother, but once again, it went straight to voice mail. She sighed and waved the waitress over.

"Look, I know you are getting ready to close. Do you know the way out to his house? He's not answering the phone and I need to get to bed soon."

"Sure. They just built a house out on the new road. There are only three houses out there now. Let me get something to write on. I'll be right back." The waitress hurried over to the register and grabbed a pad. She returned and began to draw a simple map.

Fifteen minutes later, Caitlyn was on her way with the map and a Diet Coke to go. She made it to the new road with no problems at all, but no sooner had she turned off on it, than she began having a seriously hard time keeping her eyes open. She kept her speed slow since there was no other traffic on the road. Before long, she closed her eyes and didn't open them again until she ran off the road. It jarred her enough that she hit her head on the side window. She tried to open her eyes again, but all she could see was darkness. She needed to rest. Just for a minute. She closed her eyes once again and fell asleep.

* * * *

Brody turned the truck down the newly paved road toward their equally new house. It was finally finished. Now all they had to do was find a wife. Lamar stretched his legs out in the passenger side of the truck and yawned.

"Driving to Austin to go out is a pisser if you ask me." Lamar rubbed his hands over his face. He'd had a couple more beers than Brody had. Being the designated driver meant Brody had cut off early and drank coffee the last couple of hours.

"Next time, we'll get a hotel room and drive home the next day," Brody told him.

"Still sucks to have to go all the way to Austin to find someone to date."

"There's no one in town we're interested in, what do you suggest we do? Place an ad in the Lonely Hearts section of the newspaper?"

"Hey! What's that?" Lamar pointed off to the left of the road. "Looks like a car."

"Hell, someone's gone and run off the road into the ditch. Grab a flashlight." He pulled over and set his emergency blinkers. "Let's see if there's anyone still in the car."

"Looks like they just drove into it," Lamar said.

They climbed out of the truck and walked over to where the Pathfinder sat just as pretty as you please off the side of the road. Lamar shined the light inside the vehicle and cursed.

"There's a woman in there. She's not moving."

Brody peered in through the passenger side window. He walked around to the driver's side and knocked on the window.

"Ma'am? Can you hear me?"

She didn't answer and she didn't move.

He tried the door and found that it was unlocked. When he opened the door, she moaned.

"Ma'am. Can you hear me?"

She opened her eyes and fear leapt from them. She tried scooting over, but the seat belt had her caught.

"Easy, lady. No one's going to hurt you. What happened?"

"I–I think I fell asleep. Where am I?"

"You're on Wayfill Road. Where are you trying to go?"

"My brother's house. He lives out here." She ran her hand over her face where she'd hit her head. It was tender but came away without any blood.

"Are you hurt?" He immediately grabbed a flashlight from Lamar and shined it on her face.

"Hey! That hurts."

"Sorry. You've got a bruise. Do you remember hitting your head?"

"Yeah, when I ran off the road. Look, do you know my brother? Brian Southworth."

"Yeah, you're Brian's sister? He said you were coming to the wedding. He's going to be pretty upset that you got hurt."

"Can you get me to his house? I'm really sorry to be a problem. I've been driving all night and I'm really tired."

"Where did you drive from?" Brody asked as he unbuckled her seat belt.

"Jackson, Mississippi."

Brody stopped what he was doing. He heard Lamar curse behind him.

"You drove all the way from Mississippi by yourself? When the hell did you leave?"

"Last night around eight. I had to leave. It was time to leave."

She closed her eyes and nodded off again.

"Fuck! Brian isn't here this weekend. What are we going to do with her?" Lamar asked.

"We'll have to take her to our place tonight. She's totally washed out. I'll leave a message on his voice mail about where she is. I bet he has several from her already telling him she was on her way."

"We could take her over to Tish's place," Lamar suggested.

"Tish doesn't have a spare room for her to sleep in either. She'll be fine with us. Besides, I feel responsible for her since she doesn't have anyone looking out for her. Brian is going to be pretty upset with her when he gets home."

"Hell, can you blame him? She drove all the way from Mississippi, and it sounds like she's been driving for twenty-four straight hours."

"Yeah, that was my take on it, too. Grab her gear from the back. I'll carry her to the truck."

They quickly loaded all her gear and climbed up in the cab with her in the middle sound asleep.

Lamar touched her face then shook his head. "She's awfully pretty."

"Yeah. I can see the resemblance, but she has auburn hair where Brian's is browner." Brody winced at the small bruise on her temple. He wondered if that was another reason she was so out of it. How hard did she hit her head?

He pulled into their driveway that wound a good half mile before dead-ending into their garage. He quickly unlocked the house before picking her up and carrying her into the master suite.

"You're putting her in here?" Lamar asked.

"Yeah, she's Brian's sister, and the other bedrooms don't have a private bathroom."

"If you say so." Lamar carried in her luggage and sat it at the foot of the bed.

"Think we should wake her up every couple of hours since she has that bruise on her temple?"

Lamar shrugged. "It couldn't hurt. She'll probably get mad, but we have a reason to do it."

"Ma'am, can you wake up for me for a minute? What's your name?" Brody shook her slightly.

She blinked then opened her eyes. "Caitlyn. Where am I?"

"You're at our house. Brian is out of town until tomorrow night. What's your name?"

"He's not home? But he said he would be." Panic widened her eyes. She struggled to sit up then held her hand over the bruise on her head.

"Easy. You have a bump there. Do you need something for pain?"

"I—I don't know what to do. He said he would be here."

"Easy, you're fine where you are. We live down the road from him. You're safe here. Do you want something for your head?"

"Yes, please." She lowered her eyes.

"Lamar."

"I'm on it. I'll be right back."

She finally looked directly into his eyes. Hers were the brightest green he had ever seen. They were mesmerizing. No doubt Lamar had seen them before he had.

"Here is a glass of water and some Tylenol." Lamar held both out.

"I'll help her sit up. You help her with the pills." Brody slipped behind her and held her in a sitting position while Lamar helped her swallow the pills.

"Thanks. I'm sorry I'm so much trouble."

"It's not a problem," Lamar said.

Brody smiled. His brother was smitten.

"What where you doing driving that far all by yourself?" Brody asked.

"Who else was going to come with me?" She frowned.

"I got the impression you were married or living with someone." Brody was sure Brian said she was married.

"Ah, no, I've been living with a friend, but she's getting married and needed to start getting ready for the baby. I thought I better go ahead and move out. Brian was supposed to be here."

"He didn't know you were coming, evidently. He decided at the last minute to make one more run before the wedding."

"I thought he was going to stop truck driving."

"He did, or is. He was doing a favor for someone and wanted the extra money for their honeymoon."

"I was going to house-sit for them while they were gone and start the books on their business for them."

"Brian told us you were an accountant. It's really nice of you to set up his books and help him get started. They've been working hard at the store getting it ready."

"I can't wait to see the store. He's told me so much about it." She yawned, covering her mouth with her hand. "I'm sorry. I think I need another nap."

"Go ahead and sleep, Caitlyn. I'll wake you up again in a little while to check on you."

He might as well have been talking to the wall. She was already sound asleep. Anger boiled inside him. Brian should have made sure she had someone driving out with her. She had no business being alone and certainly not driving at night. He was going to have some words with Brian when he got home.

"Uh-oh. Someone is in for it." Lamar looked up when Brody walked into the living room.

"Brian should have made sure she was taken care of before he left. She drove all the way from Mississippi alone, and did it without stopping to rest. She needs her ass paddled."

"That's Brian's call," Lamar pointed out.

"Hell, I know that." Brody walked over to the kitchen and pulled out a beer. "You might as well go on and get some sleep. I'll stay up and wake her up every two hours."

"I like her, Brody. She's special."

"Yeah, I can agree with you there, but we have Brian to deal with, and he may not like that we want to claim her."

"He doesn't know that she's separated or divorced, does he?"

"Nope, I don't think so. He sure gave me the impression that she was taken."

"Think that was just to scare off potential suitors?" Lamar asked.

"Somehow, I don't think so. I didn't think he was too happy with her husband."

"Wake me up if something is wrong. I'll be up early in the morning and then you can get some sleep if you want a nap."

"Sounds good."

Lamar left him to go upstairs to his room. All the spare bedrooms were upstairs. The master suite was downstairs on the other side of the kitchen. They had designed it that way to keep it separate from the rest of the house.

He relaxed in the recliner and sipped his beer. She was a dream come true as far as he was concerned. Between her heavenly shaped body and her beautiful eyes and hair, he would have fallen for her even without having talked to her. But listening to her soft Southern accent and the fact that she seemed so lost, he was in over his head.

Caitlyn was probably five foot three inches with rich auburn hair and the brightest green eyes he'd ever seen. She had an hourglass figure that was soft and rounded, totally feminine. He liked to have something to hold on to when he was making love to a woman.

Just thinking about her luscious figure had his cock standing up at attention. She was perfect for them. They would have to figure out how to prove it to her though. Somehow, he had a feeling there was more going on than was apparent. Anyone who would drive like she did to get somewhere had a reason for doing it. He wanted to know what her reason was.

Chapter Two

Caitlyn woke on her own for the first time and wished she hadn't. Her head hurt, and she felt as if she'd been run over by a tractor-trailer. That was what she got for thinking she could drive like she did to get to Brian's house. Brian's house! She still wasn't there. She sat up and swung her legs over the edge of the massive bed. It was big enough for three or four people.

A noise at the door startled her. The double doors opened and one of the men from the night before walked in. He was tall and lanky with just enough muscles to keep him from being skinny. He probably topped out at about six feet six inches. He had wavy brown hair and hazel eyes that twinkled as he looked at her.

"Morning. How are you feeling?"

"Um, okay."

He cocked his head and frowned at her.

"Well, my head hurts and I'm really stiff."

"You could probably use some more Tylenol and a hot bath. I'll run get the Tylenol." The he turned back and smiled at her, his eyes flashing when he did. "I'm Lamar. My brother Brody and I found you last night. I'll be right back."

He disappeared through the doors. Caitlyn stood up and winced at the tightness in her back. She really had screwed up. Brian was going to be so angry with her. What choice had she had, though? She had nowhere to go.

"Here you go." Lamar handed her a glass of water and two Tylenol pills. She downed the pills and drank the entire glass of water.

"Come on. I'll run you some water and you can soak in the tub. It will do wonders for your stiffness." Lamar led her to the enormous master bath. The tub was big enough for three just like the bed.

Silly, they probably are into ménages like your brother is. He said the entire town was different.

"Okay, make yourself at home. I'm going to cook breakfast in a little while. Have any preferences?"

"Oh, no. Thanks. I'm not really all that hungry." Her stomach chose that moment to growl.

Heat raced up her neck into her cheeks. Lamar chuckled.

"Okay, I'll surprise you." He turned around and walked out of the bathroom and then closed the bedroom doors behind him.

Caitlyn squeezed her eyes shut to stop the tears that suddenly threatened to fall. She needed to get hold of herself. She needed to be in control when Brian made it back. He would try to railroad her into something she didn't want just like Harold had. If she didn't have a plan in place, he would succeed.

Turning off the water, Caitlyn searched through her bags for clean clothes and closed herself up in the bathroom. She slipped into the tub and moaned in bliss at the feel of the warm water enveloping her stiffened muscles. It quickly lulled her into a drowsy state where nothing mattered but enjoying the feel of warmth surrounding her. Sometimes she felt as if she would never truly be warm inside again.

Harold had taken her warmth and security away from her when he admitted that he was already married to someone else in another state. All his business trips had been to see her. His job as a salesman kept him on the road a lot, but she had always trusted him. He had never given her any reason to doubt him or their marriage.

Then one day, he came home and confessed that he was already married to another woman in Tennessee. He had married her two years before he married Caitlyn. In other words, she had been living a lie for the last five years of their life. Not only that, but he had two children by his first wife and then had a vasectomy. All the time that she thought it had been her fault they couldn't have children, it had been his.

The only reason he was confessing his duplicity to her was that his first wife had found out about Caitlyn and threatened to tell her. She swallowed and buried the pain deep inside her once again. She would not let it rule her. Never again would she depend on someone else for her happiness.

She wasn't sure how long she had been in the tub when there was a knock at the bathroom door.

"Caitlyn? Are you okay in there?" She recognized the voice from the night before. He had been the one to wake her up every few hours.

"Yes. I'm fine. I'm getting out now."

"Be careful in there. Breakfast will be ready when you are."

"I'll be there in a minute." She quickly stood up and nearly fell when the room spun around her.

The door flew open and Brody grabbed her arms before she could cover herself.

"What are you doing in here?"

"You called out. I thought you had fallen."

"I–I was a little dizzy, but I'm okay now. Please leave."

Brody smiled at her and reached for the towel. He wrapped it around her and then picked her up out of the tub. When he settled her on her feet, she grasped the towel to keep herself covered.

"I'll see you in the kitchen. Just follow the hall." He turned and strode out of the room.

She heard the bedroom doors click behind him. Heat suffused her face as she fought to regain control of her breathing. He was nothing like his brother, Lamar.

Brody stood an inch or so shorter than Lamar, but where Lamar was lanky, Brody was muscular. He had strong arms and a broad chest. She would be willing to bet he was just as muscular all over with the way he moved. He wasn't hard and unbending, but she would be willing to bet that he could be that way if the need arose.

His black shaggy hair reached to his collar, making her want to grab hold of it and pull him down to her... *Are you crazy? You just found out your husband isn't your husband and you're already looking at men. Get ahold of yourself.*

Caitlyn quickly dried off and dressed before cleaning up the bathroom and repacking her suitcase. She shored up her defenses and opened the bedroom doors to the delicious aroma of cooking food. She followed the hall around to the kitchen where Lamar was busy frying bacon. He looked up and smiled at her.

"Are you feeling better?" he asked.

"Yes, thank you. Breakfast smells delicious."

"It will be ready in just a minute. Brody said you were getting dressed."

Caitlyn felt the flush of heat once again. She quickly turned away and busied herself looking around the spacious kitchen and dining area. It opened up into the den area where there was a stone fireplace on one wall and a big screen TV mounted on another wall. Several couches and recliners were scattered around the room.

"There she is. Are you ready to eat?" Brody walked into the kitchen and the room suddenly got smaller.

"I'm not real hungry."

"Nonsense. You haven't had anything to eat since you got here. That was eight hours ago."

"Here you go." Lamar set a plate on the bar in front of her. It held an omelet, bacon, and toast.

"Thanks." She watched as he loaded up another plate for Brody then himself.

They started eating, so she followed suit, but found that as good as it tasted, she really didn't have much in the way of an appetite. She managed a few bites of her omelet and the bacon, but couldn't swallow the toast. She drank the orange juice and got up to scrape her plate.

"Whoa, Caitlyn. You haven't eaten near enough to keep you going. Would you rather have something else?" Brody asked.

"Oh, no. It's very good. I honestly don't have much of an appetite this morning. Do you know when my brother will be back? I really need to get over to his house."

"He won't be back until later this afternoon. I don't have a key, or I would let you in. You're welcome to stay here though until he gets in."

"I suppose Andy is with him."

"Yeah, they always ride together."

Caitlyn swallowed and nodded. "I appreciate your letting me stick around. I'll stay out of the way."

"You're not in the way at all, Caitlyn." Brody smiled at her. "I'll show you around the house so you don't get lost.

Brody took her empty plate and stacked it with his in the sink. Lamar grinned at her as he ate his breakfast.

"I'm sure you have things to do. I don't want to interfere."

Brody made her nervous. He was so big. Yeah, Lamar was taller, but Brody just seemed to spread out in the room. She found it hard to breathe around him.

"Don't have a thing to do today. Sundays we normally laze around and watch TV. Come on." He placed his big hand at the small of her back and led her through the den.

"We'll watch something on TV later. Let me show you the rest of the house. We just moved in a month ago."

"I'm sure you're really pleased with it." She didn't know what to say to the man.

He acted as if it were important that she see the house for some reason. She doubted she would ever be back again once her brother got back home. In fact, once the wedding was over with, she would be moving on to find somewhere to settle down. She had already decided to stick to Texas so she would be close to Brian, but she didn't want to live in the same town.

"This is the office. We ought to hire you to do our books. We can't keep anything straight."

She looked at the messy desk and file cabinet. How they found anything was a miracle to her. She felt her fingers itch to get hold of the paperwork and straighten it out. It took a monumental effort not to step into the room.

"You look like you could use some help. What sort of business do you have?"

"Lamar and I own a machine shop in town."

"That must keep you pretty busy."

"We do all right." He led her from the office to the stairs.

He followed her up then showed her each of the bedrooms, pointing out his and Lamar's as well as the other two rooms.

"It's a large house for two bachelors," she said.

"We plan to find a wife someday and have a family."

"Well, you have the perfect house for it. I wish you luck."

She found herself back in the den area. Lamar was flipping through the channels on the TV when they walked in. He looked up and smiled. She felt like he was flirting with her but thought surely she was reading too much into it.

"What sort of movies do you like?" Lamar asked. "We have about anything you could imagine."

"Oh, well, you don't have to entertain me. Just pick whatever you normally would watch."

"Normally, we close our eyes and grab a movie. I'd rather you picked," he said.

Caitlyn sighed and walked over to the shelves. He was right. They had about every movie ever put on DVD. She could browse their selection for hours. She grinned and pulled out a Bruce Willis movie.

"How about this?" She handed her selection to Lamar.

"Good choice. Have you seen it before?"

"No, I've seen him in movies before, but I haven't watched anything lately."

"What did she pick out?" Brody walked back in the room.

Lamar tossed him the empty DVD case as he turned on the DVD player. As soon as the advertisements began to play, Lamar pulled her over to the recliner.

"You can watch with me. I have the best seat in the house."

"Oh, I can see just fine on the couch." She started to pull away from him, but he already had her tipped off balance so that she fell across his lap when he sat down.

"Oh!"

"Relax and watch the movie." Lamar wrapped an arm around her waist.

Caitlyn couldn't believe she was sitting in the man's lap watching TV. What was happening to her? Nothing had gone right since she had gotten up to find out that Jean was expecting a baby and hadn't told her. She had been staying with Jean for the last several months while she tried to figure out what to do with herself.

Then Jean admitted that she was getting married and the room Caitlyn was staying in was supposed to be the nursery. She decided right then that she would move out and see her brother a little early. How had she missed that Jean was pregnant?

You were all wrapped up in yourself and what was happening to you. You didn't pay attention to your friend.

Caitlyn needed a plan. Unfortunately, she wasn't going to figure one out sitting in Lamar's lap watching a movie. Despite her reservations, she soon found herself relaxing and watching the movie. They were active movie watchers. They commented on what was going on and cheered when the good guys won.

By the end of the movie, she was smiling and not the least bit worried about what her future held. Brody shoved in another DVD right behind that one and Bruce Willis once again filled the screen. Two hours later, she was laughing and joking with the brothers about the movie. Then the credits rolled and reality came crashing back on top of her.

"How about another movie?" Lamar asked.

"Shouldn't my brother be back soon?" She looked at her watch. It was closing in on four in the afternoon.

"He'll call when he gets back into town. I left a message for him." Brody pulled her off of Lamar's lap. "Come on. It's my turn to cook dinner tonight. You can help me."

"What do you want to cook?"

"How about spaghetti?" he asked.

"Sounds good to me." She moved away from him.

He kept getting in her space. She didn't think it was on purpose. He was just such a big man that anywhere he moved, he filled up the room. She watched him rummage around in the freezer for some hamburger meat. He popped it in the microwave on defrost and began to gather together the ingredients for homemade spaghetti.

She helped him brown the meat and stir the sauce until he pronounced it ready to simmer for a while. Then he pulled her back into the living room where he sat her down on the couch next to him.

"So, what are your plans after the wedding? You seem to have everything you own in your car."

Caitlyn jerked. She hadn't expected them to notice that.

"I forgot all about my car. I need to go get it off the side of the road."

"Don't worry about it. We already drove it over here. It's out in the drive."

"Oh, thank you."

"So, are you moving here?" he asked.

"No." She almost shouted it out. "I mean, I'm going to move somewhere close by so I can see my brother more often, but I thought maybe Austin. It's only a couple of hours away."

"Why not here? Riverbend is a nice community. We could sure use another accountant here."

"I—I was thinking somewhere with more people."

"You like the big city lights?" Lamar said from the other side of the room.

This time he was frowning instead of smiling.

"I don't much care about all of that. It's just that I would have a better chance of landing several accounts, so I can make a living. I don't see where I could support myself here."

Lamar stared at her for a few minutes then nodded. "Maybe, but I bet you could support yourself just fine here. Did Brody show you our office? We'd hire you. The only reason we don't use the one in town is that he's so busy he doesn't have time to take on new clients. What will your brother do once you set up his books and then leave?"

"I don't know."

She looked over at Brody. The other man was awfully quiet. What was he thinking? She couldn't see anything in his expression to give it away. Then he got up and pulled her with him.

"Spaghetti sauce should be ready. You about ready to eat, Lamar?"

"I'm always hungry."

Chapter Three

Brody's phone rang as they were beginning to gather up the dishes to wash. He answered it on the third ring.

"Brody? Is Caitlyn with you?" Brian asked.

"Yeah, she's here with us."

"Thank God. I nearly had a heart attack when I got her messages. I didn't realize my phone was dead and just charged it back up."

"We need to talk."

"Is everything okay with her? What's going on?" Brian sounded worried now.

"Everything's okay now."

"Okay. I'll be at the house in about twenty minutes."

"See you then."

"Was that my brother? Why didn't you let me talk to him?"

"He's not home yet. His phone was dead, and he didn't know it. Just got it charged back up."

"When will he be home?"

"In another hour or so. He's going to come back here and pick you up."

"Thank goodness. You've both been very nice to me, but I feel like I've interrupted your life."

"Honey, you haven't bothered us at all," Lamar said.

He flashed Brody a look. Brody nodded at him, hoping he would understand that he needed to leave. Evidently he picked up on it.

"Come on, Caitlyn, let's watch another movie till he gets here."

"Okay. One more. I haven't watched this much TV at one time in years."

Brody sat with them for about fifteen minutes, and then he slipped out and drove over to Brian's house. He and Andy had just pulled in.

"Hey, man, thanks for taking care of my sister. What's going on?"

"You tell me. I thought she was married?"

"She is. Is something going on with her marriage?" Brian frowned. "Why are you asking me all of this anyway?"

"She drove from Jackson, Mississippi to here nonstop, Brian. By herself. We found her sound asleep on the side of the road."

"Ah, hell, Caitlyn." Brian ran a hand through his hair. "Something's going on then. She wouldn't have done that unless she was desperate."

"How was she getting here before you left on your trip?" Brody realized that Brian really didn't know what was going on.

"She was driving with her husband. They were supposed to arrive the day before the wedding and she was going to stay and house-sit while she set up the books for the store."

"She's lucky to be alive, Brian. She's planning on moving to Austin, I think. She had everything already packed inside her car."

"Like hell she will. She'll move here where I can watch out for her. I never would have left her in Mississippi if she hadn't been married. Not that I liked her husband all that much."

"Lamar and I want to claim her." Brody watched Brian's face.

His expression stiffened, and then he ground out, "What in the hell are you doing with her at your house, Brody?"

"Stand down, man. We're not doing anything. She's running scared, Brian."

"I don't know that it will do you any good. I can't see her going for a ménage relationship, and if she's hurting, it's not the time for you to be approaching her."

"I know that, but we want you to know where we stand. We're claiming her."

"Fuck." Brian's jaw worked. "She's my sister, man. You're asking me to let you fuck her."

"Well, not right away, but she needs something, Brian. Let Lamar and I figure out what it is she needs and give it to her."

"I want to see her first. Then I'll make up my mind."

"She's going to expect to stay with you here," Brody said.

"And if she wants to, she can," Brian said, looking Brody in the eye.

"Fine. I told her you would be by to pick her up when you got in town. Give me a few minutes to get back over there then come on." Brody walked out of the house and drove back to his place.

He'd been sitting watching TV for about ten minutes when the doorbell rang.

"That's probably Brian." Caitlyn jumped up from the couch where she and Lamar had been sitting.

"I'll get it," Brody said.

He got up from the recliner and answered the door. Brian and Andy both stood there. He let them in with a nod and watched to see what happened.

"Brian! I'm so glad to see you." Caitlyn threw herself into his arms.

Then she pulled back and smiled at Andy. Holding out her hand she introduced herself.

"You must be Andy, I'm Brian's sister, Caitlyn. It's a pleasure to meet you."

"Same here, ma'am."

"Please don't ma'am me. I'm older than he is but not much."

"You're older than Andy? I thought he was your big brother," Lamar said with a grin.

"Nope, he's my baby brother by two years." Caitlyn continued to hold on to Brian as if her life depended on him.

"What are you doing here without your husband?" Brian asked, getting down to business.

"He's not my husband anymore. It's a long story. Maybe we should go to your house."

"Caitlyn, did you drive all the way here without anyone with you? Do you know how dangerous that is?"

"Don't start with me, Brian. You have no idea." Her voice grew cold and distant.

Brian sighed. "Fine. Let's go home and you can tell me what the hell is going on."

"I really appreciate everything the two of you did to help me." She turned to Lamar and Brody.

"It was our pleasure. You have to let us show you the town while you're here," Lamar said.

"Where are your things, Caitlyn? I'll get them," Andy offered.

"I'll show you." Lamar led Andy out of the room.

"Andy's going to drive your car back to my place. You can ride with me."

"I'm sorry if my coming so early has caused a problem, Brian, but I really didn't have a choice."

"Nonsense. You're not any trouble. If I realized you were coming, I wouldn't have taken that last haul. Everything will be fine. You'll see." Brian wrapped his arm around her once more and pulled her in for a hug.

When Andy returned with her suitcases, they walked outside and loaded up. She climbed in the cab of Brian's truck and Andy took the keys to her Pathfinder from Brody and followed them to the house.

Brody watched them until he couldn't see the taillights anymore. Then he walked back in inside and filled Lamar in on what he'd found out.

* * * *

"Caitlyn, what in the hell is going on?" Brian asked when they were settled in the living room with a beer.

She looked over at where Andy sat across from her and back at Brian expectantly.

"He stays. We have no secrets in this house, Caity." Brian reverted back to her old nickname.

"I'm not married."

"You got a divorce?"

"No, I never was married. The bastard already had a wife in Tennessee." There. She'd said it.

Total silence.

"That son of a bitch! How did you find out?" Brian was instantly on the couch next to her holding her close.

"He told me. His *real* wife found out about me and threatened to tell me, so he came clean." She didn't even shed a tear now. It was as if all her emotions had vanished now.

"Caity, baby. Why didn't you call me to come see about you?"

"I'm a grown woman, Brian. You had your new relationship, and I didn't want to screw that up for you. I handled it. I moved out and stayed with Jean. Then when you invited me for the wedding and to house-sit, I figured that was the perfect time for me to move on."

"What made you decide to come on ahead of time?" Brian asked.

Caitlyn hesitated, but at his lifted eyebrow, figured she might as well come clean. She told him about Jean being pregnant and getting married.

"I just thought it would be okay for me to come on ahead of time. I'm sorry I busted in like this."

"Nonsense, you are always welcome here."

Andy sat on the other side of her. "There will always be a place here for you, Caitlyn. You're family."

"Thanks, Andy. I appreciate it. You don't even know me, and now I'm jumping in like this. I promise, I'm usually better organized."

"Don't worry about it. You've had a shock. Brian, I'm going to go put her things in the guest bedroom." Andy stood up and walked over to where they had set her suitcases when they first walked in the door.

"Thanks, man." Brian squeezed Caitlyn's hand. "Caity, we'll get everything worked out."

"There's really nothing to work out. If the offer still stands, I planned to stay here while you are gone on your honeymoon and set up your books while I house-sit, and then when you get back, I'm moving to Austin and starting over. I'll be close by so we can visit."

"I'd rather you move here so I can help if you need it. I won't be able to see about you all the way in Austin, Caity." Brian looked worried.

"I can take care of myself. I'm twenty-eight years old, Brian. I'll find a place to live and move in and find a job. I have plenty in savings to cover a few months if it takes a while."

"Why don't you plan to stay here until you find a job, then move. That way you can pick out a place close to work that is what you want."

Caitlyn sighed. He was going to be a bear about it. "I'll think about it. I have time before I have to decide what to do."

"You take all the time you want to. There's plenty of room here. I can't wait for you to meet Tish." Brian's face lit up at the mention of the woman's name.

"I feel like I already know her. You've talked nonstop about her for weeks now." Caitlyn smiled.

She was so happy for her brother. He'd had a brief live-in back in Mississippi that had not worked out at all. The woman had nearly killed him with her manipulative behavior, pitting him against his friends. As much as Caitlyn hadn't wanted him to leave her, she had been glad when he'd moved and found a place where he was happy.

He had driven through Riverbend on one of his long-distance trucking trips and fallen in love with it. He told her the people were very open and honest there. It had sounded like just the place for Brian and his freethinking ideas. Trust him to decide to live in a ménage relationship. He had assured her that there were several in the town.

"She will be so excited to meet you. She's going to be the one taking over the books after you set them up. You know me and paperwork."

"So tell me more about your store. I know it's new age, but what all will you have in it?"

Brian filled her in on the type of merchandise and the clientele they expected. He already had a mail-order business and needed her to help him sort that out as well.

"I'm so proud of you, Brian. You and Andy and Tish will do wonderfully. Setting up a website and running mail order first is what will increase your sales. How much of a mess do I have to fix from that?" she teased.

"About three months' worth." He winced at her rolling eyes. "Had I known you were free all that time, I would have already had you out here setting it up."

"Well, there's nothing for it. I'll get it set up for you. You can show it all to me tomorrow. I might as well get started on it. Is everything at the store?"

"Yeah. We don't officially open until the first of next month, but we've been doing a little selling here and there, and of course, the mail order. Um, do you mind keeping it up while we're on our honeymoon?"

"Of course not. I'm sure I can handle it."

Andy spoke up as he entered the room. "Would you like another beer, Caitlyn?"

"No, thanks. I probably better get to bed. I need to get an early start in the morning. What time do you plan to go in to work?"

"Nine." Brian stood up and stretched. "Does that sound good to you?"

"I'll be up and ready. Want me to fix breakfast?"

"Nope, that's Andy's specialty. He does most of the cooking."

"Do you have any preference?" he asked her.

"No, thanks."

"I'll show you to your room." Brian grabbed her hand and pulled her down the hall.

"What did you think of Brody and Lamar?" he asked when he showed her the bedroom.

"They were very nice to me. You have some good friends."

"So you liked them?"

Caitlyn stared at him. "Yeah. Why?"

"Just wondering. I'll see you in the morning. Hope you sleep well, Caity."

Caitlyn closed the door and looked around the small room. It wasn't as large as the guest rooms at Brody and Lamar's house, but it was nicely decorated and would be fine for as long as she would be staying.

She took a quick shower in the attached bathroom and settled down for the night. The bed was comfortable, but sleep wasn't in her future, it seemed like. She had slept in so late that morning.

She thought about Brody and Lamar and wondered if they were still watching TV or if they had gone to bed. She didn't know what time they would go to work at their machine shop. Stifling a yawn, she lay back and contemplated her life. Starting over in Austin seemed like the best idea, but she wondered if staying in Riverbend wouldn't be just as good.

No. You worked this out, Caitlyn. You need your independence, and if you stick around Brian, he'll run your life for you. No, she was better off moving to Austin.

Thoughts of Lamar and Brody intruded into her thoughts. She had really liked them. She had to admit that they had piqued her interest. Just being around them had kept her wet, which was more than she could say about her ex-whatever-he-was.

She sighed. They seemed like nice guys. But she wasn't in the market for nice anything right now. She had a life to get on with and starting over didn't include starting a new relationship. Not now and probably not ever again.

Chapter Four

Tish was already at the store the next morning when she and the guys drove up. Brian's fiancée was beautiful to say the least with her long blonde hair and baby-blue eyes. She had a delicate air about her that belied the spirit beneath the surface.

Tish embraced her and immediately began regaling her with tales from their recent past and how the three of them had met.

"Let me show you the office and you can get comfortable. I'm so excited you're here so early! We can have so much fun without the guys tagging along."

"Don't count on that, Tish. You're not allowed to run off without telling me where you're going," Brian called out.

"Is he serious?" Caitlyn laughed.

"Unfortunately. Around here, the men take their job of seeing after their women very seriously. You'll see. Wait 'til you want to do something, and he doesn't want you to."

"Sorry, but I'm my own woman, and I'm two years older than him."

Tish rolled her eyes. "That's not going to make a bit of difference. You'll see." She changed the subject. "I hear you met Lamar and Brody. What did you think about them?"

"They're very nice. They helped me when I was totally out of it. I still can't believe I fell asleep driving. I was so lucky." Caitlyn shook her head.

"Yeah, you were. I'm surprised Brian hasn't said anything to you about it."

"I think I shocked him with my marriage fiasco. He can't handle more than one issue at a time. Typical male."

They laughed over that and began to sort through the invoices and paperwork for the business. Several hours later, Brian knocked on the door and produced drinks. He had her much-coveted Diet Coke.

"Thanks, Brian. You're an angel."

"So, is it a total mess or can you fix it?" he asked.

"Well, it's a total mess, but I can fix it. And Tish seems to have a good handle on it, so I don't foresee any major problems. I can do your taxes for you, your quarterly estimates and all. That won't be a problem."

"Great! You really ought to open an accounting business here. There's only one other accountant, and he doesn't have time to take on new clients." He grinned at her. "Think about it, at least."

"Get back to work, Brian, and leave us women alone." Tish pushed him out of the office and closed the door behind him. "Don't mind him. He just wants you close by. He said you were looking to move to Austin. That's only two hours away, so you wouldn't be too far."

"That's what I keep trying to tell him." Caitlyn rolled her eyes.

They worked in the office for another couple of hours and then broke for lunch. They all went over to the diner and ended up sharing a large table with Lamar and Brody.

"How are you doing today?" Lamar asked her.

"Hey, Lamar. Hi, Brody. I'm doing fine. Working on setting up their books."

"We've been talking and wanted to hire you, if you have the time, to set up our books. We've been screwing around with them for several years and they're a mess. Maybe if you set them up right to begin with we could keep them up." Brody's intense gaze bored into her.

"Oh, well. I'm not sure I'll be here long enough, but maybe I can give you some easy pointers to get you headed in the right direction."

"That would be great. We'll take what we can get," Brody said.

They laughed and discussed the weather, the state of the nation, and local news. Caitlyn tuned it all out and noticed how many tables contained two men and one woman. One even had three men sitting with a single woman. Were *they* in a relationship?

Lamar leaned over and whispered in her ear. "That's Jessie and her men, Gordon, Harry, and Michael. They have a little boy named Timothy."

"They look really happy. I didn't mean to stare."

"It's natural to be interested in what's around you. You'll find that most of the families here are ménage. The few that aren't have other *different* viewpoints such as D/s relationships."

"You're kidding." She looked around and thought she had one picked out by the way the woman kept her eyes down.

"Some wear collars and some wear bracelets."

Brody was sitting on the other side of her. He took her hand and squeezed it.

"What is Lamar filling your head with?"

"He's just pointing out that people here live by their own laws."

"Yeah. Does that bother you?" Brody asked.

"No, I think it's great that they can all get along and live like they want to. It's unusual in a small town. Maybe you might see these kinds of relationships in a large city, but not usually in a small community like Riverbend."

"Well, the entire town is made up of odd relationships. The mayor and his wife are in a D/s situation. The majority of the town council live in ménage relationships. It's more the norm than the exception."

"That's really great."

"Think you might like to stick around?" Lamar asked.

"I don't know. I really think I would be better off in Austin. Living this close to my brother probably isn't a good idea."

"I think it's a great idea. You need someone to help you, and living two hours away will put a strain on Brian," Logan pointed out.

"He shouldn't have to help me out at all. I can take care of myself."

"Maybe someone else would like to take care of you for a change. You shouldn't have to worry about the day-to-day stuff. You should just enjoy life." Lamar seemed to be trying to tell her something, but she wasn't sure what.

Caitlyn listened to the conversations around her and thought about how relaxed everyone seemed. She wanted that feeling again, but didn't know if living there would be the answer or not. She didn't want to be under Brian's thumb. He was already bossy enough, and if what Tish said was true, he would be worse.

Austin was a progressive town. She would be fine there. She could visit anytime she wanted to. They had the spare bedrooms and an occasional long weekend would do her good. He would have his hands full with a new marriage and the new business. Brian wouldn't have time to worry about her. Brody and Lamar were wrong there. He wouldn't need to worry about her living in Austin. She could take care of herself.

"You ready to head back?" Brian's voice broke into her thoughts.

"Hmm? Yeah." She started to get up and Lamar was immediately there helping her up.

"Have a good afternoon, Caitlyn."

She smiled at him. "Thanks. Bye, Brody."

She followed the others out of the diner and back toward the store. She couldn't get Lamar's remarks out of her head that maybe she should let someone else worry about things for a change. Would she ever be able to trust anyone again enough to let down her guard? Caitlyn wasn't sure she would.

* * * *

Lamar watched her leave with the others. He sat back down with Brody moving to the other side of the table.

"What?" he asked.

"We don't have a lot of time, brother. She'll be here for the next three weeks. If we don't convince her to marry us before then, we'll have to go back and forth to Austin and court her."

"If we don't convince her before she moves to Austin, little brother, we've lost out. She's not going to change her mind once she leaves here where everyone is relaxed about sharing."

"Then we've got to work fast and hard. I can't imagine my life without her, Brody. She's perfect for us."

"She's just getting out of one marriage. I don't see her jumping into another one anytime soon."

Lamar wiped a hand over his face and huffed out a breath. "What do you suggest we do? Give up without even trying?"

"No. I'm just saying this isn't going to be easy."

"Nothing worth having ever is, Brody. We both know that."

Lamar knew what was eating Brody. He didn't like that there was an ex involved. The last woman they had been serious about had an ex and eventually went back to him. Brody had been pretty messed up over that and hadn't wanted to date anyone right out of a relationship because of it. He didn't trust that they wouldn't jump right back into it.

The fact that Caitlyn was married or recently divorced bothered Brody. If he hadn't already gotten attached to her, Lamar had no doubt that he wouldn't even be considering her. She would have been off limits as far as he was concerned.

He watched Brody for any sign of what he was thinking. The other man was a master at hiding his feelings behind a hard exterior that few could break through. If Lamar wasn't already half in love with Caitlyn, he wouldn't force his brother's hand, but he was. She was the one for them. He knew it in his heart and felt it in his soul.

"I'm willing to try, Lamar, but I'm not getting my hopes up. She can change her mind just as easily as she can make it up."

"She's not like Cindy. She's been hurt, too, Brody. Give her a chance."

"So had Cindy, Lamar. We were there to pick up the pieces and she still went back to that son of a bitch."

"Forget about her. All that matters now is Caitlyn. Where do we start?"

Brody sighed and leaned back in the chair. Lamar could tell that he was torn between wanting her and not wanting to go through the pain of rejection again. It had hurt Brody far more than it had hurt him. Brody had thought she would be a good wife for them. It had hurt his pride that she'd chosen the douche bag over them.

"Well, we have Brian and Andy's shelves about ready. Let's take one of them over tomorrow and see if it works. We can talk to her some more and see how she is doing."

"Good idea."

"Maybe we can convince her to let us buy her dinner."

"We can take each of the shelves over there on a different day until she agrees to go out with us." Lamar nodded. "I like that."

"Let's just hope that Brian is still okay with us courting her. We don't know what the circumstances are behind Caitlyn's marriage breaking up. If he changes his mind, we've got a fight on our hands."

"He won't. He knows we'll take good care of her."

"I hope you're right." Brody stood up and dropped several bills on the table for the tip. Then he took the ticket and headed toward the cash register.

Lamar followed, pleased to see that Mattie was at the register. She and her husbands Nate and Bruce owned the diner.

"Hey, Mattie. How are you all doing?"

"Fine. Business has been brisk lately. How are you boys doing?"

"Been busy as well." Brody nodded.

"Brian's sister is quite a good-looking woman. What do you think?" Mattie grinned at Lamar.

Brody grunted, but Lamar answered her. "She definitely is."

"Thinking about courting her?"

"We're thinking about it, but she's talking about moving to Austin instead of here. We've got our work cut out for us."

Mattie nodded. "Looks like you might need some help to convince her she'd rather live here."

"We'll take all the help we can get." Lamar waited while Brody paid their ticket.

"Good luck, you two. It's about time you found someone to settle you down."

They waved and walked through the door outside. Lamar followed Brody over to the truck and climbed in without saying anything. He could tell that his brother wanted to say something but was weighing his words first. Usually when he did that, it was important. Lamar hoped it wouldn't be anything that they would end up fighting about.

The made it back to the shop and had been working for nearly thirty minutes before Brody finally spit it out.

"If she's still married, Lamar, I'm backing off. I'm not getting mixed up with a married woman. If you're still interested in her once her divorce is final, I'll be willing to court her then, but I'm not messing with a married woman."

Lamar had to count to ten before he threw the part he was working on across the room. Fuck, Brody! He should have known he would figure out a way to put a hold on it. He had been thinking too much about Cindy.

"Don't say anything, Lamar. You know I'm right."

Lamar could feel his blood pressure rise. It didn't help that Brody was right. He hadn't planned on her being married. He had been hoping she was divorced already. Maybe it had been wishful thinking, but he wasn't going to give up.

"We can still be friends with her until her divorce goes through," Lamar managed to get out through gritted teeth.

"I guess we can as long as you draw the line at anything physical. No kissing, Lamar."

"I hear you loud and clear, Brody. Fuck! Just forget about it for now."

Lamar didn't want to forget about anything, but if they were going to keep from arguing the rest of the day, they needed to back off of the subject. He sighed and finished the motor part he'd been working on. Tomorrow was a new day, and he couldn't wait for it to get there.

Chapter Five

Caitlyn laid down the pencil and rubbed her eyes. Then she keyed in the final figures on the spreadsheet and hit save. One down and half a dozen more stacks to go. She was slowly plowing through their invoices and entering them into a database for them to use to track their sales and run reports. The spreadsheet was mainly for her. She wanted to keep track and make sure the database worked so she was using it as a tick-and-tie method.

"How are things going, Sis?"

"Slow, but they're really going well. The database is working just like it's supposed to. I'll keep the spreadsheet until I leave to be sure the other doesn't have any glitches in it. You don't have to keep up with both of them. I feel sure it will work great for you."

"You don't know how much I appreciate this, Caity. The accountant here in town didn't even have enough time to spare for a lesson. I sure wish you would think about moving here. You would have more business than you would know what to do with."

"Brian, I honestly don't think that it would be a good idea. I like the sound of living in Austin. I would be close enough to visit on a regular basis but far enough away that we wouldn't get on each other's nerves."

"And I'll worry about you all the time. You'll be alone without anyone you know to help you if you need it. What happens if you lock yourself out of your house or car?"

"I'm a big girl. I'll deal with it. You can't live my life for me. Yeah, I screwed up, but that doesn't mean I'm not capable of making decisions."

"I never said you couldn't make decisions, Caity. Just think about it, all right? I can't help but want you close. We're all either of us has left."

"That's not true anymore, Brian. You've got Tish and Andy now. You're building your own family."

"It doesn't mean I don't need you. You're my sister."

Caitlyn sighed. Brian wasn't going to give up. Part of her really wanted to stick around Riverbend. It seemed like a nice place from what she had seen so far. But part of her knew that staying close to Brian would mean that he would try to run her life.

So, aren't you strong enough to say no if you need to? Why move so far away when you could live close enough to watch his family grow?

Thoughts of Lamar and Brody intruded into her mind. She tried to push them back out. She didn't need to even think about another relationship right then, maybe never. She obviously had poor taste when it came to men. What made her think that they were any different?

A clanging noise toward the front of the store jostled her from her thoughts. She wondered what was going on, but didn't bother getting up from the desk. Brian and Tish were out there. If something was wrong, they would call out. She continued working on the files she was entering into their new database.

A few seconds later, the door next to the office opened and Brody backed into the storage area in the back of the store. He was carrying one end of a metal storage shelf of some type that looked as if it had been custom made. As he disappeared farther into the shop, Lamar emerged with the other end of the thing followed closely by Tish, Brian, and Andy.

"Okay, put it over there against that wall. That's it." Tish had no trouble directing the men where she wanted the rack.

Once it was in place, they stood back and admired their work with Lamar grabbing a drill off one of the counters and proceeding to secure it in place.

"It looks perfect. When will the other two be ready?" Tish was fairly bouncing with excitement.

"We'll bring one over tomorrow and the other one on Thursday," Brody told her.

"Caitlyn, come look at our custom-made shelves." Tish indicated the impressive assembly. "Lamar and Brody weld, and they're making our shelving units for us. It was going to cost an arm and a leg to get just the standard ones shipped, and then we were going to have to put them together."

"These are cheaper, better made, and already come assembled." Brian grinned at her.

"Well, they do for some people, anyway." Lamar chuckled.

She walked out of the office and admired them. They were well made and looked like they would be perfect for the type of merchandise that they carried.

"I'm impressed. They fit the store perfectly and have all the bells and whistles, too. That holds shipping paper, doesn't it?" She pointed out the spool that was mounted on the end of the unit.

"That's right." Brody grabbed a roll of paper and demonstrated how it worked.

"The two of you would really rack up the sales for stuff like this in a bigger city."

Brody's facial expression grew tight. "We don't want to live in a big city. We like Riverbend just fine."

For some reason, Caitlyn felt as if she'd hurt his feelings.

"I don't blame you for wanting to live here. It's a perfect little town. I don't really like all the traffic and hordes of people either."

"Then why move to Austin when you can easily move here? You already have all your stuff with you." Lamar jumped in when Brody remained silent.

"Austin isn't as large as some cities, and it has a smaller-town feel to it. I just think that living so close to Brian would be asking for fights," she finally admitted.

She didn't see why they were so interested in her moving to Riverbend. They barely knew her. They had spent a day together, but it didn't mean they were best pals or anything. She still would have wanted to move to Austin despite their being good friends just to assure that her brother didn't jump in her business. Speaking of which, she needed to go through the finances and make sure she had covered all her bases, and Harold hadn't gotten away with anything other than pulling the wool over her eyes.

"Gee, thanks, Sis." Brian crossed his arms and frowned at her.

"You know it's true. You like to boss me around, and I like to ignore you."

"Those are typical brother-and-sister actions." Tish wrapped an arm around Caitlyn's waist. "My sisters and I don't get along when we're around each other too much."

"I'm sure Brian is only looking out for your best interests," Brody pointed out.

"Well, he tends to get a bit too involved with my personal life, though."

"If you had listened to me, you wouldn't have married Harold in the first place."

"Brian!" Tish's shout wasn't in time to prevent him from cutting Caitlyn to the quick.

She ground her teeth together and walked toward the front of the building.

"I'm going to take a walk around town. I'll be back later."

"Caitlyn…"

"Don't, Brian. You've said enough." She kept walking until she was outside and heading toward the middle of the little town.

There were several shops on both sides of the street she hadn't looked at and several empty buildings as well. She walked toward the little department store down the block. She could spend some time in there while she calmed down.

"He didn't mean to say that, Caity." Lamar walked up on one side of her while Brody took the other side.

"I didn't ask for your opinion, and I didn't ask for company."

"Well, you've got both." Brody stopped her with a hand on her shoulder. "Why are you so upset?"

"Why am I so…He effectively said I told you so and did it in front of virtual strangers." She refused to cry.

Tears pricked at the back of her eyes despite her willing them to stay away. What were they doing following her anyway? She was just a friend's sister. If anyone should have followed her it should have been Brian or Andy.

"He didn't mean to hurt your feelings, Caity. He's cursing himself back there now."

"No, Tish is cursing him. He doesn't see that he said anything wrong. Don't try and tell me how my brother is feeling. I've known him a lot longer than you have."

She pulled away from Brody and continued toward the department store. She didn't expect them to continue following her, so when one of them opened the door to the store, she stared.

"What?" Lamar asked with a grin.

"Why are you still following me?"

"Because we're trying to get up the nerve to ask you out to dinner tonight."

"Why?" She could only stare at them even harder now.

"We want to get to know you better before you leave."

"I don't get it. What's the point?"

"We like you, and with Brian living here, you're bound to visit him on a regular basis." Lamar grinned.

"And you want to see me anytime I'm here. If I say yes, will you behave?"

"Define behave." Lamar seemed to be doing all the talking.

Somehow, she figured there was a reason for that. She narrowed her eyes at Brody. He was watching her with hooded eyes. If she didn't know better, she would say he was horny. She couldn't help but drop her eyes, and sure enough, the outline of his cock was apparent against his jeans. Her mouth dropped open, and she jerked her eyes back up only to find a knowing smile there. She felt her insides melt as her panties grew wet with her arousal.

"Maybe we should take this over to our shop where we can talk without being overheard." Lamar wrapped his arm around her shoulders and pulled her out of the doorway and farther down the sidewalk.

"W—we don't have anything to talk about."

"Sure we do." Brody's hand went to the small of her back as they ushered her along.

"Like what?" She looked over at Lamar and found he had the same knowing smile on his face.

"How about the fact that you're soaking wet right now, and I'm hard as a fucking rock."

She stopped walking and stared at Brody as if he'd just admitted to being a Martian. She couldn't believe he had the nerve to talk that way to her. They didn't even know each other for God's sake.

"Come on, Caitlyn, you don't want to have this conversation in public." Lamar took her hand and pulled her around a corner.

After a few more steps, Brody stopped and unlocked a building that looked like a warehouse. She looked around before they herded her inside. She didn't recognize anything around her. She hadn't been paying attention to where they had been heading. How would she ever make it back to the store?

"Don't worry, baby. We'll make sure you get back safe and sound—after our talk."

"What talk?" She turned to Brody.

He backed her against Lamar with his body. She should have been frightened, but for some reason, she wasn't scared of him. She was turned on and pissed off, but not frightened. When he lowered his head to hers, she could have turned away, but she didn't. All she could think about was the intense need in his dark eyes.

When his mouth touched hers, she opened instinctively. Greedy lips sipped at her lower lip then sucked at it. His tongue caressed hers before exploring the rest of her open mouth. He devoured her from the inside out then nipped around her jaw to her earlobe.

Lamar was the steady rock behind her that kept her from melting from the onslaught of sensations Brody created with his hot mouth. He whispered naughty thoughts in her ear as his brother licked and nipped along her neck.

"Your pretty pussy is creaming for us, isn't it, baby? I bet if I put my hands down your jeans right now they'd end up wet and tasty."

She couldn't answer him. Brody's mouth had her gasping for breath as he seared a path from her jaw down her neck. When his teeth closed over one clothed nipple she nearly screamed. Her breasts ached to be touched. Her nipples had pebbled in reaction to his earlier kiss. Now they burned for more stimulation.

Caitlyn couldn't believe she was reacting to them like this when she barely knew them. She hadn't even gotten half this hot with Harold in all the years she'd been with him. What was going on with her?

Brody stared deep into her eyes as he pulled her T-shirt up to her neck. Then he pinched her nipples with his fingers through the thin layer of silk that encased them. She couldn't stop the shudder that ran through her body. Neither could she stop her body's reaction when he pressed his aroused cock against her belly. She moaned and pushed back.

"I can smell your sweet cunt, babe. You're driving me crazy. I want inside that pussy so badly it's about to kill me." Brody leaned into her as he spoke.

Lamar ran his hands around to cup her breasts in his hands. He moaned in her ear as he massaged them through the material of her bra. Brody went to his knees and began to unfasten her jeans.

"What are you doing to me?"

"Making you feel good, baby. Just relax and let us show you how well we can take care of you." Lamar kissed the side of her face near the corner of her eye.

Brody slowly shoved her jeans and panties over her hips and down to her ankles. Then he nudged her feet as far apart as they would go with her jeans in place. She gasped when he blew a warm breath across her waxed pussy.

"She's bare, Lamar."

"Fuck! How does she taste?"

Brody leaned in and ran his tongue up her slit, gathering her juices as he did. He lapped at the bounty and growled low in his throat.

"She tastes like honey." He licked again.

Then he reached up and took her hand, running her finger through her wet heat.

"Let Lamar taste you, babe."

Lamar took her wrist and drew her finger to his lips. He sucked it into his hot mouth and swirled his tongue all around the wet digit.

"Hell, yeah. She tastes better than honey. I could lick your hot pussy all night long."

"Please, I can't stand it. It's so good." Her legs trembled as the two men teased her pussy with their fingers.

Brody buried his face between her legs and began to suck and lick his way around her mound. When he entered her with two fingers, she nearly screamed at the glorious sensation of his thick, callused fingers thrusting into her cunt. His tongue continued to torment her pussy lips then swirl around her clit. The dual sensations had her blood heating in no time.

When Lamar pushed her bra up over her breasts, releasing them to his attentions, she whimpered and thrust them deeper into his hands.

As he licked and nipped along her jaw and neck, he pinched and pulled on her bare nipples. She loved the slight pain as he took it just a little past teasing and into the darker side of pleasure. She had always enjoyed things a bit rough, but Harold had never wanted to explore anything beyond the missionary position.

A hot flame licked at her cunt as Brody's fingers cupped and found her hot spot. He rasped his rough fingers over the spongy tissue often enough to send her senses into overdrive but not enough to send her into orgasm. She sobbed out a breath when he pulled back from the sensitive tissue to thrust deep into her over and over. Then he licked a quick slide of his tongue over her clit, getting her attention.

"Let us take you out tomorrow night, Caity." Brody lapped at her clit twice more, earning him a hissed-out *yes* and a squeeze of her legs around his hand.

"You're bribing me, or are you blackmailing me?" She had a difficult time speaking around her heart in her throat as he rasped his fingers over her sweet spot once again.

"We're doing whatever it takes to get a *yes* out of you, baby." Lamar pulled her nipples out far enough that she almost took a step closer to Brody to ease the tension.

Again, Brody licked over her clit and rubbed at her G-spot. Then he pulled back slightly and looked up her body into her heavy eyes. She knew in that moment that he wanted an answer before he went any further. Would he leave her unfulfilled, antsy, and needy? Somehow she didn't think he would, but he would draw it out. She licked her suddenly dry lips. She was seriously considering letting them take her out.

"Okay. I'll go with you."

Brody hummed his approval against her pussy before latching on to her clit with his teeth and thrumming it with his tongue. He shoved his fingers deep into her cunt then pulled back and tapped at her hotspot all at the same time.

Between Brody's assault of her pussy and Lamar's rough treatment of her breasts, Caitlyn didn't stand a chance. She exploded into a thousand pieces with pleasure that she'd never felt before. Nothing had ever prepared her for the unbelievable sensations the two men stirred inside of her. She held on to Brody's head with both her hands to keep her grounded. Without that tie, she was sure she would have flown away.

Even as the intense feelings of pleasure burned through her, unease settled in behind it. What had she done? She looked down at herself and took a shaky step back from the two men. Dear God. She had just found out that her husband wasn't her husband and already she was acting like a loose woman.

Chapter Six

"Easy, Caitlyn. Everything is fine." Lamar held his hands out away from his body.

He had felt the minute she had become aware again of what she was doing. Tension rolled off of her like steam off of hot pavement after a refreshing rain. Evidently she hadn't found it as refreshing as he'd hoped.

"It's not fine. I just let the two of you make me come, and I haven't known you more than a couple of days."

"You enjoyed it, Caitlyn. Don't try and tell us you didn't." Brody was on his feet standing in front of her as she struggled to pull her panties and jeans back up.

Lamar moved her hands away and helped her fasten her jeans. He hated seeing her this upset over something that had been so good for all of them. Watching her come and knowing he'd had a hand in helping her to let go had been amazing. He wanted to do it again. Instead, he was helping her dress so that she could pull away from them.

"I can't help it that my body has the morals of a loose woman."

"Don't ever call yourself that again." Brody backed her into Lamar again.

"Then why did I just make out with two strangers not even two months since I found out my husband isn't really my husband? Can you answer that?"

"Yeah, you belong with us," Brody said.

Lamar nearly winced. This was not the time or the place to throw that at her. She wasn't going to take his announcement well.

Sure enough, Caitlyn went completely still before slowly turning toward Brody. Fire fairly leapt from her eyes as she zeroed in on him. Lamar almost felt sorry for his brother. Almost.

"I don't belong with anyone. I'm not some object to be owned by anyone, much less the two of you. Neither of you know jack crap about me, so how can you stand there and profess that I belong with you? You know next to nothing about me or my life."

"Then give us a chance to learn." Lamar was desperate to know more about her.

"Since you agreed to go out with us tomorrow night, we'll start there." Brody crossed his arms and stared down at her.

"I changed my mind."

"Nope. Can't do that."

"I most certainly can."

"So you're telling me that you're going back on your word. In other words, we can't trust you."

"Ooh! You are driving me insane. Don't you get it? I'm not interested."

"I beg to differ, babe. You were more than interested a little while ago. Don't add lying to the mix."

Caitlyn looked over at Lamar. He just shrugged. She needed to work this out for herself. As much as he wanted to soften Brody's words, he was right. She agreed to go out with them, and he was with Brody on not letting her back out of it. It was the only way to learn more about her and show her that they would be good for her.

"Fine. I'll go out with you." She sighed and turned to walk across the room toward the door.

Lamar hurried to the door and opened it for her. "Where are you going?"

"Back to the store. I need to finish what I was working on."

She sounded so dejected that Lamar wondered if they hadn't pushed too far. As happy as he was that she was going out with them, he didn't want to lose the passion and spirit from earlier. He touched her shoulder.

"What's wrong, Caitlyn?"

She stopped just outside the door and drew in a deep breath.

"I'm not used to anyone telling me what I'm going to do or how to feel. I've basically been on my own for a very long time. Harold wasn't home a lot, so I had only myself to rely on. I don't know how to be any different, Lamar. I'm not the woman for either of you, much less two of you." She continued walking toward Main Street.

Lamar didn't say anything. He figured he should just keep his mouth shut and steer her in the right direction. When they got to Main Street, he urged her left then right, down Elm. He stopped and opened the door to Brian's store and followed her inside. Once he was sure that the men were there, he would back off and leave her alone. She was going out with them. That was a good first step toward their goal of making her theirs.

Brian walked out of the back and sighed when he saw her. He walked up to her and started to hug her. She took a step back, putting her lower back on Lamar's rock-hard dick. She stiffened but didn't move.

"Caity. I'm sorry. I shouldn't have said what I did."

"Why not? You meant it. You never did like Harold and tried to get me not to marry him from the beginning."

"He was too slick—oily. I figured him for a player and not good enough for you."

"And you were right about him being a player."

Lamar listened, trying to put two and two together. So far he figured the bastard had lied to her and cheated on her. What had she meant about him not being her husband? Were they or weren't they married? If she wasn't married, that cleared the way for them without a messy divorce to wade through.

"I'm really sorry, Sis. I never wanted you to get hurt. That's why I want you to move closer to me. I'd watch out for you. I know you can take care of yourself, but why do it all when you have a brother who can help?"

"You're about to have a new bride who needs all your time. I don't want to interfere. If I moved here, you'd be torn between your home and me because you can't stand it unless you're nosing around in my business."

"I'm not that bad, am I?"

Lamar felt her stiffen. Evidently she thought Brian was always being nosey.

Brian sighed and planted his hands on his hips, hanging his head. When he looked back up, his expression looked tired and worried.

"Sis, at least think about it. Stay for a few weeks and get to know everyone. You'll find out that they're all friendly and great to be around. You never know, you might meet someone you like."

"Brian, I hardly think I'm going to do that. I just got out of a mess. I don't need to jump feetfirst into another one."

Lamar had to backpedal when she suddenly took a step back to turn and walk around her brother. He watched her disappear into the back room with her back straight and her head high. She had her pride, and Brian had embarrassed her in front of them. She wouldn't forgive him for a while. He figured the man had some groveling to do. He'd been out of line.

"I don't know what I'm going to do if she moves off to Austin. I can't watch out for her there and handle my life here." Brian ran a hand through his hair.

"Leave her to Brody and me. We'll take good care of her and convince her to move here."

"She's going to move as soon as we get back from our honeymoon. I would extend it another week, except that we need to get back to officially open the store and see about the online orders."

"What if we help her run the mail-order side of the business and you do the grand opening in another month? Could you stay gone for two weeks then?"

His eyes gleamed for a few seconds. "Let me do some checking, and I'll let you know later tonight. How's that?"

"Sounds good to me. Oh, she agreed to go out with us. I'll call her later and firm up when."

"You're kidding. She actually agreed?"

"Well, I'll admit we sort of backed her into it, but hey, all's fair in love and war."

* * * *

Caitlyn spent the rest of the afternoon concentrating on getting her brother's books set up and ready for business. Then she started on unraveling the mess he'd made of his online business. He had the support needed to put them in order, but it would take some time to get it all entered and up to date. Then she would need to teach the entire setup to Tish. That would mean after they got back from their honeymoon. So, she figured another three or four days, so she might as well as make it a week before she moved. All she had waiting on her in Austin was a hotel room and the want ads.

That thought dampened her spirit even more. She wasn't one to mope about things. She got busy and took care of them instead. Only right now, she wasn't in any position to take care of anything. Maybe her best bet was to look for a job first and then, once she found one, move into a place close by. And Riverbend was a nice community. Several people agreed that they needed another accountant. She shook her head and stood up to stretch.

"Hey, Caity. I was getting ready to call it a night. Tish has supper ready if you are."

She drew in a deep breath and nodded. After shutting everything off, she followed Brian out the door to the truck.

"Did Andy leave with Tish?"

"Yeah, it's just been the two of us all afternoon."

"Don't you worry about them being alone together so much?"

He laughed. "You still don't get it, do you?"

She shook her head as he climbed up into the cab of the truck. She really didn't see how two men could love the same woman and not get jealous of the other one. Like now, why wasn't Brian worried that his best friend and Tish were alone together all afternoon while he had been stuck at the store with her?

"We both love her, Caitlyn. I know that if anything were to happen to me, Andy would be there to take care of her and the same if something happened to Andy. I know that they spend time together alone. She and I spent an entire weekend together when he went to settle some business with his family a few months back. It's how things are in a ménage relationship."

"So what happens when you walk in on them?"

"Do you mean making love? Do I join them or walk off?"

"Well, yeah."

"It depends. If it's something that they obviously need, I just walk away knowing that they are reinforcing that part of themselves that is there for each other. If it looks more like fun, then all bets are off." He waggled his eyebrows at her.

"TMI, little brother."

"You asked." He grinned at her and then sobered. "Just think about all the love, support, and help Tish has between the two of us. She doesn't have to work if she doesn't want to. She will always have one of us to lean on when times are rough. Wouldn't you like to have that, too, Caity?"

"We're not talking about me. We're talking about you and your family."

"Which you are a part of, as well."

"Fair enough. If it works for you, then that is all that matters. I'm glad you found what you have, Brian. I'm not judging at all when I say I just don't think living this close to you would be a good idea. We have always been at odds over things in life, and I don't see that changing. I don't want to live in the same city and have fights all the time over little stupid things that blow out of proportion."

"I agree. I was hoping that we had grown past that. I'm really sorry for what I said earlier. It was out of line in front of people you don't know that well. I probably shouldn't have said anything at all."

"You think?"

"Yeah. I think." He grinned over at her as he pulled into the drive.

She didn't even think to check if the lights were on at Brody and Lamar's house when they passed by. Why did it matter anyway? God, she had to stop her mind from drifting in their direction every chance it got. She was not interested in them no matter how attractive or attracted to them she had become. They were quite honestly man candy, and she hadn't been around so many good-looking men in a long time. They had to breed them that way there in Riverbend.

As they walked into the living room, Andy stood up from where he'd been lounging on the couch in front of the TV.

"Hey, Tish has dinner just about ready. You've got time to freshen up if you want to though."

"Thanks. I think I'll do that." She left the two men exchanging wordless expressions across the room and headed toward the stairs.

A quick shower would be wonderful. She thought about ducking her head into the kitchen and asking Tish if there was time for one but decided at the last second not to. She could wash her face and change tops to a cleaner one that didn't feel like a year's worth of grime had fallen on it.

Or the four hands of two very virile men hadn't touched it only hours earlier. I've got to get them off my mind for at least a few hours.

As it was, she managed to change her top, rinse off, and repair some of the damage to her makeup from earlier before they called her down to dinner. She felt somewhat more like her normal self throughout the meal. They discussed everything from the business to the little town itself.

"We've been looking into extending our honeymoon for another week, Caitlyn. Would you be able to stick around for another week with us? We would put off our grand opening by two weeks into next month so you wouldn't have much to do other than deal with the mail-order side. Lamar and Brody agreed to help with carting anything off to the post office or UPS if you needed help." Tish's enthusiasm was so contagious that Caitlyn didn't have the heart to tell them no.

What would it hurt to be there a little longer? She didn't have anything waiting on her. She was keeping busy with the books and now would have the mail-order business to run as well. She could take more time to determine where she might want to work. She would snag the Sunday newspaper to scope out possible job opportunities in Austin. Maybe she would look at the rental situation here in town as well. It wouldn't hurt to look.

Ten minutes later, she was helping Andy clear the table when her cell phone rang. She jerked, not used to hearing it ring, before grabbing it and answering.

"Hello?"

"Hey, Caitlyn. It's Lamar."

"Hi." She almost asked him what he wanted, but refrained from being so rude.

"I just wanted to firm up our plans to go out tomorrow night. Nothing fancy, just a meal and maybe dancing afterward."

Caitlyn's mouth opened to say no then closed with her remembered promise. She had to keep her word. She didn't back away from a challenge nor did she go back on her promises.

Chapter Seven

Lamar listened to the hesitancy in Caitlyn's voice. She really wanted to say no to their date, but she wouldn't back out of it out of pride. She kept her word. He admired that about her. When some women would have exercised their right to change their mind, she hadn't. And then on some level, Lamar liked to think that she really was attracted to them on a deeper scale.

They had a sexual chemistry without a doubt, but there was so much more to life than just sex. You couldn't have a true ménage relationship without a sexual glue, but neither could you have a permanent relationship of any kind without more than sex, either.

"Dancing?" Caitlyn's voice broke into his thoughts.

"Yeah, depending on how we're feeling after dinner. We could relax at the bar down from the diner and maybe dance a little. You know, get to know each other a little bit. We are really serious about that part, Caity."

"I don't get why when you know I'm planning to move once they are back from their honeymoon."

"I guess we're hoping the friendly people and nice town will help change your mind. Besides, if nothing else, you'll be back to visit and it would be fun to have someone to go out with occasionally when we're in that direction. We usually go about once or twice a month right now."

"Brody seems a little more *attached* to the idea of my belonging to you two. I don't need a man to tell me how to feel or think."

Lamar sighed, knowing this was going to come up sooner or later. Brody had really stuck his foot in the mess when he'd made that announcement to her. She was coming off a bad relationship, and clearly Brody was steering them down the same road in some form or fashion.

"He didn't mean it like it sounded, Caitlyn. He just means that he thinks we're perfect for each other. He doesn't know any other way to talk except in affirmations. You say something enough and believe it enough, and then it becomes real."

"Why would he want us to be an item when he hardly knows anything about me? I could be a real shrew. Hell, by now, he probably already thinks I am."

Lamar laughed. "You're no more a shrew than Tish is. You've been through a lot in the last few months and your entire life is up in the air right now. I can understand that you need some time and some help. Let us help you, Caitlyn."

"I just don't see what's in it for the two of you."

"The chance at a wonderful woman with the possibility of forever in her eyes. That's what's in it for us, Caity. Just say yes and we'll pick you up tomorrow at seven. Nothing fancy needed. Just wear jeans and a shirt and maybe some dance shoes."

Her softly indrawn breath was all that told him she was still on the line several seconds later. Finally she let her breath back out and answered him.

"Okay. I'll see you two at seven tomorrow night. Don't be late or I might change my mind after all."

"Never, Caitlyn. One or both of us will be there on time to collect you. Sweet dreams."

Lamar didn't even wait to hear her surprised response. Instead he ended the call with a click of the button and slipped his phone back in its holster before going in search of Brody to tell him the good news.

"What are you smiling about?" Brody looked up from the desk where he was sorting through invoices.

"Just got off the phone with Caitlyn. We're going to pick her up at seven tomorrow night."

"You're kidding. She didn't back out?"

"Nope. She wanted to, though. You're going to have to back off some with her, brother, or she's going to run to Austin before we can get her to change her mind."

"She pushes all my buttons, Lamar. I'm trying. I wonder if Brian has said anything to her about lengthening their honeymoon yet." Brody leaned back in the desk chair clasping his hands behind his head.

"Yeah, I think he has. She was already a little on edge when she answered the phone. I'm sure that's going to be something we need to be careful talking about as well, or she'll put two and two together. She's not dumb."

"Hell, no. She's probably about the smartest woman we know. Maybe we can inch her toward helping us with our books some, as well. I noticed that she gets all bright eyed and lost when she's working. She might start putting ours together and not want to just leave in the middle of the mess. It could buy us some more time with her."

Lamar grinned. He liked that idea. "I'll push it at her without being overbearing. You leave that part to me."

"I want to know what is going on about her marriage or divorce or whatever it is. We need to know what we're up against. You know Brian isn't going to tell us. It's her business."

"You can talk to her about that. Just remember to not be pushy about it. Try and be sympathetic so she'll want to talk to you about it."

"Lamar." Brody gave him a wry look.

"Yeah, you're right. You're not very sympathetic about things, but you can pull it off. Just think about how hard this is on her and how much she's suffered because of it. Don't think about the bastard you want to tear apart. Think about the woman you want to make happy."

"I guess when you put it that way, it makes it a little easier."

"Good. Now what is going on with that Brisswick project we bid on? You sounded pretty pissed off on the phone."

"Seems that they were told we did shoddy work on the city's fence section that was replaced after old man Phillips ran into it last Christmas."

"We didn't do that section of fence!" Lamar kicked at the desk leg.

"That's what I told them. They hemmed and hawed around about who had told them we had. I never did find out, but they are going to rethink their decision to keep their business in town."

"Someone's trying to cause problems for us for some reason. Who have we pissed off lately?"

"I don't think we've upset anyone in a long time. Maybe it's all just about business and they are *hit below the belt* type players. We don't work that way, but a lot of people do."

Lamar shrugged. "More than likely it came from whoever did the stupid fence for the city in the first place."

"Well, I'm not going to sweat it if we don't pick up this bid. We're more than covered for time anyway. Plus, now I want any spare time we can get to use on persuading Caitydid to give us a chance."

* * * *

Caitlyn spent the entire morning finishing up the books for the mail-order side of Brian, Andy, and Tish's business. Once she had them set up and clean, she spent the afternoon going over them with both Brian and Tish. Andy ran the errands and answered the phone. By five, she was exhausted but pleased at all the progress. She was confident that Tish would be able to handle the books just fine. Brian would be a good backup, but he wasn't as interested in numbers.

She sighed and peeled off her clothes to get in the shower. She was almost looking forward to the evening now. She needed a little downtime away from her brother and his new family. She just wished it wouldn't be with two men who were bound and determined to date her. Hell, who was she fooling? They were dating her. She was going out on a date with them tonight.

After showering and drying off, Caitlyn sifted through her clothes and settled on a pair of navy blue slacks with a red blouse and low-heeled shoes. If they planned to take her out dancing, she better be ready. They seemed to be the type to keep her on her feet all night. Maybe that was their ploy. Keep her on her feet so that later she would be happy to get off of them. She smiled and shook her head at that dirty little thought.

As much as she could see them using every advantage in their arsenal to get her to let down her guard, she couldn't see them keeping her dancing all night in an effort to tire her out for sex later. The sex would be mediocre at best if she was that tired.

By the time the men arrived to pick her up, Caitlyn had changed into the comfortable outfit and was just putting on a little makeup so she wouldn't look washed out. She followed the sounds of masculine laughter downstairs to find the four men standing by the front door talking.

"There she is." Lamar stepped out from the others and took her hand. "Ready to eat?"

She let him pull her toward him and Brody without a hassle. She liked being near them, maybe too much.

"I could definitely eat."

"Let's get going then." Brody opened the door and held it as Lamar escorted her out.

She caught a glimpse of Andy and Brian grinning at each other and frowned back at them but didn't get a chance to say anything as she was hurried toward the men's truck parked in the drive.

"Are we late?"

"No, just don't want to miss any time we have with you, Caitydid," Brody said with a strained smile.

She turned to where Lamar was climbing up in the truck next to her. The other man didn't look as relaxed as usual either. What was up with that?

"Is something wrong? You're both awful tense about something."

Lamar and Brody exchanged glances. Neither man offered to explain so she crossed her arms and glared straight ahead. She wouldn't get out of the truck until they explained what was going on. She was sure it would involve her since they were both tense.

"Did Brian say anything about extending their honeymoon by a week or so?" Lamar finally caved and spoke up.

"Yes. I think it's great they are going to spend more time together before getting back to real life. It has to be difficult forging a relationship between three people."

"I don't know about that. I think they already have a great relationship. I just think they should have the time to relax before getting back to business." Brody frowned at her. "Do you think a relationship between three people would be all that much more difficult than between two?"

"Brody, one thing at a time." Lamar turned back to Caitlyn. "Did he tell you that we would be around to help with the mail-order part so you don't have to haul packages back and forth to the post office?"

"Well, he said you might help some with the heavy stuff. I can handle the small things, so I doubt I'll really need your help that much."

"You don't have to go to the post office at all if you don't want to. Brody and I will carry all the packages for you. All you have to do is wrap them and get them ready for us to pick up."

"I like going to the post office. I have to pick up their mail anyway to keep up with bills and orders and such."

"We'll work it out later." Brody was obviously ready to end the conversation as they pulled up in front of the steak house.

Lamar helped her down again and they walked in and were seated at a secluded table in the back. The waitress took their drink orders then left them to deliberate over the menu. Since she had never eaten there before, she pored over the offerings. Everything sounded wonderful.

"What do you suggest? It all sounds great to me."

She must have caught them by surprise when she asked for their help because they stared at her for a several long seconds before answering her. She rolled her lips inward to hide her smile.

"The steak is always good here, but if you want something lighter, there is the fish." Lamar grinned at her as he pointed out her choices.

"Fish sounds good to me. Salmon or snapper?"

"Snapper," Brody suggested.

"Great. I'll have that and a baked potato."

By the time the waitress had returned with their drink order they were ready. Brody ordered for her and remembered to ask what she wanted on her salad. She couldn't fault their manners or the way they seemed determined to make sure she was comfortable. Harold had never really been all that concerned about her comfort.

She cleared her mind of him and that time. It was over with. She had made a terrible mistake in marrying him. Well, not that they had actually been married, after all. She still hadn't come to terms with that aspect of the ordeal. She had never been married to the bastard at all. Legally, she was a free woman, but she still felt married to some extent. It probably explained why she wasn't exactly comfortable going out with Lamar and Brody.

The food arrived and she was glad to pour her concentration into eating. It was really very good. She was pleasantly surprised having expected that being outside a large city, the food wouldn't be quite up to par. After having eaten at the diner though, she should have known better. Everything in Riverbend seemed to be excellent, the shops and the food.

"How is the snapper?" Lamar asked.

"Excellent. It has a great flavor."

"I've only had it once, but I remember it being pretty good." Brody took a bite of his steak. "You should try the steak next time though. It's really good. All of the meat is raised right here in Riverbend."

"I'll have to do that one night when I'm really hungry. It was just too heavy for me tonight."

"Well, I for one am glad you're not going to be too full to enjoy some dancing." Lamar grinned over at her. "I can't wait to dance with you."

"I'm not much of a dancer. I haven't really danced in years."

"You'll do fine. You're naturally graceful." Brody leaned back in his chair and nodded at Lamar. "He'll wear you out on the floor though if you let him. Just let me know when you're tired and I'll rescue you."

Caitlyn smiled. She liked seeing the playful side of Brody. He was more intense and brooding than Lamar.

"I don't suppose you would have some time tomorrow to go through our office with us and give us some pointers, would you?"

"I'm actually about caught up on Brian's mess. I could start looking at yours tomorrow after lunch." She couldn't believe she had agreed to do that so easily. Had she had more to drink than the single glass of wine?

"That would be great. We really need all the help you can give us. We've had to take our taxes to Austin each year since there's no one here with time to work on them. It's costing us a lot of money because we aren't very, um, organized." Brody's brooding nature was back.

"I'll see what I can do to help. The thing is, you need to keep on top of it or it will get out of hand in only a few days or weeks."

"Riverbend could really use another accountant." Lamar made the observation this time.

She drew in a deep breath but refused to let them bait her. She wasn't going to get into the middle of that discussion with them again.

They took care of the bill and Lamar escorted her to the truck.

"Can't wait to get you on the dance floor, Caitlyn. This is going to be fun."

She wasn't so sure, but she was game to find out. It had been a long time since she'd had fun going dancing. Would it unnerve her to be with two men in public like this? It hadn't bothered her at dinner. Would it be any different at the bar dancing?

Chapter Eight

Brody and Lamar carefully maneuvered Caitlyn around the bar toward the empty table in the back of the room. Brody could feel the beat of the music all the way to his soul as it thrummed at the base of his spine. His balls were already sensitive to the nearness of Caitlyn, but the promise of rubbing bodies with her had them even more aware. He wasn't sure how he was going to be able to behave with her so near to him.

"How's this?" Lamar asked as they stopped by the empty table.

"Looks fine to me." Caitlyn took a chair and they crowded around her.

Brody was relieved to see that she didn't balk at them getting closer to her at the table.

Ether she really was okay with there being two of them dating her or she wasn't thinking about it right then. Of course, it helped to live in a town where the norm was to be different. Most of the others in the bar were part of either a ménage or a D/s relationship.

"What would you like to drink?" Lamar leaned toward Caitlyn to be heard over the music.

"Oh, whisky sour would be fine."

Lamar nodded at him and walked toward the bar to get their order. He and Lamar drank draft beer. He looked around. The dance floor was already full, and there were people at the bar almost two deep now.

"So what sort of computer program are you using for your books?"

"Program? Um, I guess we aren't using one. I just have everything in an Excel spreadsheet. It's not great, but it works. Sort of." Brody winced.

Actually, it wasn't working, but he hated to admit it even to her. He just wished she would agree to marry them and they could live happily ever after, at this point. He'd admit to screwing the books up and just about anything else if it would put them closer to convincing her to stay and give them a chance.

"Uh, spreadsheet? You don't have Quicken or Bookkeeper?" She had an odd expression on her face. Then she shrugged. "Okay. We'll figure out what sort of program you need and get it."

"Sounds good to me. Just tell me what you want, and I'll get it for us." Brody was all about making her happy.

If a stupid computer program would help his cause, he'd get it. Hell, he'd drive to Austin and get it if need be. Then, if they had to wait for it to arrive via mail, she would be around them longer waiting on it to come in. He liked that idea even more.

"What are you smiling about?" A wary expression covered Caitlyn's face.

"Just happy to finally have you here with us."

She looked as if she were going to say something, but Lamar returned to the table with their drinks.

"Taste that and be sure it's okay, Caitlyn. The bartender made it so haphazardly that I'm not sure it's what you ordered."

She took a sip of the drink and smiled. "Perfect."

Lamar shook his head and took a drink of his beer. "I'm surprised. They're swinging bottles around like on that movie *Cocktail*. It's a wonder they haven't dropped something yet."

Brody loved the tinkle of her laugh. His cock stirred at the sound. He was going to have to control that monster or risk pissing her off. But, hell, he couldn't help that she turned him on with just a smile. He had no doubt that she could crook her finger and he'd be all over her like a puppy on its momma.

"Okay, time to dance." Lamar stood up and held out his hand to Caitlyn. "You coming, Brody?"

Caitlyn hesitated when Lamar asked, so he shook his head. "I'll sit this one out. Have fun."

He saw her visibly relax at his reply to Lamar. Maybe being with two of them did bother her, after all. Or maybe just the idea of dancing with him bothered her. He would figure that out later when he danced with her. Right now, he needed to relax some or that moment might not come.

The sight of Caitlyn and Lamar circling the dance floor had his heart sputtering. They looked good together. Finally, they centered in one spot that was easily visible to him. He watched as Lamar ran his hands up and down her arms then circled to rest just above her hips on either side. Brody's groin tightened again. Fuck! He'd never be able to dance with her if he didn't lose the damn hard-on.

When Lamar kept her out on the dance floor for another go, Brody finished off his beer and snagged a waitress for another one. Maybe it would help control his libido some. Alcohol was supposed to be a downer.

"That was fun." Caitlyn returned with Lamar and took a sip of her drink.

"Want another one? That one is probably a bit warm." Brody started to flag a waitress.

"No, thanks. It's fine." She waved a hand in front of her face. "Whew, it got hot out there."

"Yeah, I got hot myself." Lamar was obviously not talking about the temperature.

Brody hoped his brother knew what he was doing. They weren't supposed to be pushing her too hard, and Lamar seemed to be doing some pushing. Well, if little brother could do it, so could he.

"As soon as you've caught your breath, it's my turn."

She chuckled. "I must be a glutton for punishment. Let's go."

Brody exchanged a quick grin with Lamar. She was having fun. Either she hadn't had a lot of opportunities to in the past or her ex-whatever-he-was had suppressed that in her. What he wouldn't give for five minutes alone with the guy. Then he remembered Lamar's suggestion and concentrated on Caitlyn and making her happy.

He pulled her to her feet and steered her toward the dance floor with a hand to the small of her back. He realized how small and delicate she was. His entire hand covered her lower back. Next to her, he felt like an overgrown, hormonal teenage boy intent on getting to first base.

He pulled her into his arms and was thankful for the slow dance and the opportunity to just hold her close to his heart. He had little doubt she could feel the bulge that was his erection pressing into her from beneath his jeans. She didn't say anything, but he knew when she'd touched it with her belly. Caitlyn's back grew straighter and her body began to stiffen up.

"Easy, Caitlyn, it's a natural reaction when I'm around you. It doesn't mean anything other than that I'm attracted to you. I'm not going to throw you on the floor and ravish you—unless you ask me to."

"It's sort of difficult to ignore, Brody. It's so, um, big."

He chuckled. He knew he was large, but it always helped his ego for a pretty woman to comment on it.

"What is so funny?" Her face twisted into a frown.

"Nothing. It's just that there is no way I'm going to lose the boner with you complimenting how big I am."

"Oh." She turned a soft, pinkish red at his comment.

He pulled her tighter into the cup of his arms and body so that they no longer brushed suggestively against each other's body.

The music had just slowed down to the beginning of another song. Brody decided they'd had enough and, wrapping an arm around her waist, directed her back toward their table.

"Thanks, I enjoyed that."

"It was all my pleasure, I assure you. Rest up before Lamar claims another dance. He really is insatiable in some things." He waggled his eyebrows at her.

When she laughed that tinkling sound again it left Brody's heart in a flutter, fighting to get back on rhythm. He could easily see himself working to hear her laugh on a regular basis. She was going to have them both wrapped around her finger when they finally managed to win her heart.

"So what would you rather do, Caitlyn? Own your own business or work in an office for someone else?" Lamar asked.

"Well, I'd rather have my own business, but that takes a lot of work to get started and if you don't have a rather large nest egg when you start, you can end up in trouble rather fast."

"If money wasn't a problem, would you go ahead and do it?"

"Probably. It's potentially more lucrative to have your own office, but often hard to get started in. You have to gain the respect of the community before they will trust you, especially where money is involved. People are a lot less trusting in the accounting business."

"True, but you have a readymade business here if you were to stay."

She smiled and shook her head. "How do you figure that?"

"Well, you've got Brody and I, your brother, and I'm sure there will be others who are taking their books to Austin or maybe even to Cooperville."

"Some people want the big name behind them. It breeds security that they will win should they end up in an audit."

"You'd be surprised how many don't feel that way around here. We're a close-knit community. We take care of each other, worry about each other, and support each other's businesses." Brody jumped in.

"That's all fine and good, but it still doesn't convince me that I could make a go of it here, and there is still the matter of my brother living within nosey distance."

Lamar laughed at that but Brody frowned. He already knew that was the major sticking point with her. She didn't want anyone to boss her around. They had to figure out a way to convince her that he wouldn't be doing that in reality. That job would fall on his and Lamar's shoulders.

Lamar stood up and held out a hand. He was ready to dance again. Brody stood up with them and followed them to the dance floor. Once again, Caitlyn didn't balk at there being two of them with her. They sandwiched her between them and danced to a fast tune before it changed to a slow song. Then they both held her between them as they rocked to the rhythm. Lamar placed his hands on her shoulder with one wrapped around the back of her neck while Brody settled his hands on her hips. They didn't do anything suggestive or lewd. They just settled into a nice swaying rhythm and held her.

* * * *

Caitlyn let them hold her as they danced to the heart-wrenching love song. She knew both men were horny from the feel of their rather impressive packages on either side of her body. She wasn't sure, but she thought Brody had been that way since dinner. Who was she kidding? She was just as turned on as they were. Still, it didn't mean she should jump into bed with them. She barely knew them.

Then there was all their talk about opening her own office. They hadn't said in Riverbend at first, but she was sure that was where they were talking about all along. When she had brought it up, they had quickly defended the small town as being protective and supportive of their own. Would they consider her an outsider though? Probably not since she was Brian's sister.

"What are you thinking about so hard?" Lamar asked looking down into her eyes.

"Sorry. I didn't mean to space out on you. I guess I got too relaxed."

"That's a good thing," Brody said from behind her.

"But not very nice to my boyfriends." She stumbled when she realized what she'd said.

Boyfriends. Am I really thinking about them as my boyfriends? I don't know them that well.

"Your boyfriends are happy, so don't worry." Lamar brushed a kiss against the corner of her eye just as the music ended.

She let them lead her back to their table. No one had taken it, amazingly enough. Since she had finished her drink earlier, she didn't have anything to hold on to at the table. She clasped her hands in her lap and waited on the guys to decide what they wanted to do. Would they call it a night or suggest another round? She really didn't mind staying, but she figured it was a work day the next day for them especially. She was only doing paperwork, so getting a later start wasn't that big a deal for her.

"Would you like another drink or do you want to call it a night?" Brody asked.

"Um, well. I'm game to stay, but we really should call it a night since it's a work day tomorrow."

"Sounds good." Lamar got up and held the chair for her to stand up.

They escorted her through the throng of people where the heat of the building gave way to a softer temperature outside. Despite it not being chilly, Caitlyn shivered at the difference between the two. Brody wrapped an arm around her shoulders, drawing her in closer to him.

"Cold?"

"Not really. I think it was just the difference in the temperatures between outside and inside."

"I can understand that." Lamar walked on the other side of her.

Once they arrived at the truck, Brody released her to Lamar and unlocked the truck. They climbed in with her in the middle and headed out of the parking lot. Sitting between the two of them soon had her antsy. She couldn't control her arousal as her pussy gushed juices at the close proximity she was to their still-engorged cocks. She was hyperaware of Brody's hand on her knee and Lamar's draped across the back of her shoulders along the seat back.

"Where are we going?" She finally managed to concentrate on where she was.

"I thought we'd go back to our house and talk for a little while. We're only down the street from your brother's. We'll get you home by midnight. We all need to be in bed by then." Brody didn't apologize for making the assumption that she would go along with his plans. He pulled in to their drive and got out.

Lamar helped her out of her seat belt and out of the truck while Brody unlocked the door. Caitlyn wasn't too sure this was a good idea, especially considering how her traitorous body was reacting to being so close to them. She had little doubt that all it would take would be a few kisses and caresses and she would end up in bed with them.

Would that be so bad, Caitlyn? They're clean, handsome, and obviously hardworking men. You could do worse. I can't think this way. It hasn't been long enough since I found out about Harold.

She argued with herself as she let the men lead her into the living room and settle her on the couch between them.

"I'm going to make some coffee." Lamar got up and walked into the kitchen leaving her alone with Brody.

"What time do you want to stop by and work on our mess of a bookkeeping system?"

"Maybe right after lunch would be a good time. Can you take the time to show me what you have then?"

"No problem. I'll meet you here at one."

"Sounds good. I should have everything that needs doing at the store finished by then."

Brody leaned in and gently kissed her lips. Before she could think to say stop, he had deepened the kiss and her body was going along come hell or high water. Her muscles relaxed into his embrace and her nipples hardened into little round pebbles, scraping against the material of her bra. The added sensation only made her moan as he encircled her in his arms. At some point, she had lifted her arms to rest her hands on his shoulders. She kneaded them like a kitten did its mom.

He sucked in her lower lip and ran his tongue along it before nipping it and again soothing the sting. His mouth ate at hers before sliding down to leave kisses all along her chin and jaw on his way to her ear. There he sucked in her earlobe, drawing on it as if he was dying of thirst and it was a fountain.

It wasn't until he began leaving openmouthed kisses along her neck and shoulder that she realized at some point he'd unbuttoned her blouse and shoved it down her arms. It stilled her in his arms for a few seconds, then his kisses and gentle caresses seduced her back into the moment, and she realized she didn't want to stop. For the first time in a very long time, Caitlyn was excited about sex and actually turned on. She wasn't going to cut off her nose to spite her face.

When Brody pulled back and searched her eyes, she made sure he saw that she was more than just okay with his seduction. She slipped her arms from the sleeves of her blouse and pulled his head down to hers for another kiss. It was his turn to moan this time as she explored his mouth with her teeth and tongue.

The couch dipped beside her and Lamar joined them. His warm hands cupped her shoulders as he pushed in behind her. He made short work of delivering her from the confines of her bra. Then he covered her breasts with his hands and began massaging them lightly with his palms.

She pulled her mouth away from Brody to lean back against Lamar, thrusting her aroused nipples deeper into his hands. He chuckled behind her and began to pluck at them with his fingers. Their callused roughness stimulated her to the point that she began to squirm between the two men.

"Lamar, we need to move to the bedroom. There's not enough room on this couch for what we want."

The second they pulled away from her she whimpered and reached for Brody. She didn't want to stop. He pussy was already soaking wet. She had little doubt that her slacks were stained with her copious juices. To her relief, Brody reached down and picked her up in his arms. He carried her toward the stairs.

"I can walk, you know. You'll never get me up those stairs. I'm too heavy, Brody."

"You're not heavy. I've got you, Caitlyn. Just relax and don't choke me. If you do, all bets are off."

"Lamar! Make him put me down."

"Not happening, babe. He's got you."

By the time she had appealed to Lamar, Brody already had her almost to the second floor. She buried her face in the crook of his neck and shoulder as he stepped up on the landing. Then he was hurrying into the master bedroom with her. She yelped when he dropped her on the bed with a bounce.

"Let's get these pants off of you, Caity. They're in the way." Brody knelt on the floor and pulled off her shoes as Lamar unfastened her slacks.

Once they had removed them along with her underwear, Brody settled between her legs as Lamar lay on his side next to her. Caitlyn shivered with the first touch of Lamar's mouth on her shoulder as he licked and nipped his way down her arm. He crossed over to her breasts and began torturing her with his tongue at her nipple without really applying the pressure she wanted and needed.

Brody garnered her attention when he sucked in her pussy lips. He tugged on them as he stripped them of her juices. She squirmed as he pulled back and began to lick at her slit from top to bottom. His raspy tongue tickled and stimulated her to the point of digging her fingers into the covers beneath her. She wanted to hold on to one of them, but wasn't about to get in their way as long as they were busy taking care of her.

Lamar began lightly twisting one of her nipples, and she moaned, wanting more. She was just about to let him know when he nipped at the other one making her forget as the pleasure-pain swamped her senses. Then Brody garnered her attention when he thrust two fingers inside of her as he continued to devour her around them.

Between the two men, Caitlyn couldn't catch her breath. They totally manipulated her in the way they wanted her to go until she was beside herself with pleasure. When Brody swiped his fingers over her sweet spot, she hissed out *yes* loud enough for anyone in the area to hear. Lamar chuckled around the nipple he was sucking on.

Brody redoubled his efforts, mercilessly dragging her climb to the top out until she thought she would die from the buildup. Her body ached to climax. Every nerve ending was alive with need. She finally got the energy to speak and all but begged for release.

"God, Brody! Lamar, I'm on fire. I need more!"

"Easy, Caity. We'll take care of you. Feel for us." Lamar pulled on her nipple long enough to reassure her, only it wasn't very reassuring at the moment.

Finally they took mercy on her. How they were able to coordinate it, she didn't have a clue, but just as Lamar pinched one nipple while teething the other one, Brody latched on to her clit and sucked. He continued to stroke her hot spot.

Wave upon wave of heat coursed through her veins as pleasure overtook her senses. She had nowhere to go to get away from the intense sensations bombarding her body. She burned from the inside out and felt the wave carry her up, up, up until there was no air to breathe. Then she was free-falling into nothing but ecstasy.

She was barely aware of Brody donning a condom and positioning himself at her opening. Then his thick cock breached her pussy and tunneled through her swollen tissues in an effort to fill her.

"Fuck, she's tight. God, baby, let me in."

"You should have seen her face, Brody. She looked like a tormented angel when she came."

Caitlyn moaned as Brody thrust inside of her over and over until he reached her cervix. He stilled, leaning over her to catch his breath. She looked up to see his head was thrown back and a look of intense concentration across his face. She could tell that he was trying to keep from coming too soon. She rolled her lips into her mouth and held them there with her teeth as she squeezed her cunt muscles around his cock.

"Aw, hell. Don't do that, Caity. I'm barely holding on as it is now. I want to enjoy this, make it last."

"Move, Brody. I need you to move."

He slowly pulled nearly all the way out before slamming back inside of her, using his dick as a battering ram. She whimpered and raised her body to meet him. They fucked each other as Lamar sat back and watched them. Caitlyn was having none of that.

"Don't just sit there staring, Lamar. Play with my tits and I'll play with your balls."

"You don't have to do that, baby. I'll take care of you. I just had to watch Brody take you for the first time." He nipped at both nipples before alternating sucking on them.

This time when her orgasm began to build, she was ready for it, or so she thought. The thundering in her ears only added to the sense of the unknown. When the pleasure bordered on pain, Caitlyn threw her hands up and grabbed Lamar's head, pulling it down for a kiss. She desperately ate at his mouth, needing that personal touch to become the catalyst to shoving her into the pleasure of coming. A tidal wave of pleasure poured over her body, making every muscle contract as she spasmed around Brody's cock.

As her pussy squeezed his dick, she heard him shout out his own orgasm, filling the condom with hot cum. He fell over her, catching himself on his hands before he suffocated her. Lamar moved out of the way just in time. It barely registered at the time that Brody was talking until her ears stopped ringing.

"…you're the best thing that's ever happened to us, Caity."

She shivered at his words, knowing that things wouldn't turn out the way that he wanted. Then he was pulling out of her, holding on to the condom, and Lamar was taking his place.

"Please tell me you're not too sore."

"Just don't expect me to come. I'm climaxed out for the night."

"Baby, you're going to come if I have to fuck you all night."

She threw back her head and growled. They were going to kill her. Two times was a record for her. Hell, one time was never a sure thing, anyway. If they knew how special it was that she'd climaxed twice, they'd use it against her in their bid that she was perfect for them.

Lamar slowly entered her pussy with his sheathed cock. He didn't hurry by any means. Instead, slow and steady seemed to be his style. He tunneled in and out of her cunt painstakingly slow until she squirmed, needing more. He grinned and began to increase the pace. It was then that she realized her body was gearing up for another round of pleasure. How could that be true? Surely there was no way she could reach that pinnacle three times in one night. It just wasn't possible, was it?

"Hell, Caity. Your sweet pussy is dragging at me like it doesn't want me to leave. Do you want more? I can give you more."

"Yes! More. I want all you have, Lamar. I need more."

He took her at her word and began to pummel her cunt with his cock, rasping over nerve endings with white-hot sensation. At the end of each shove of his dick, he bumped her cervix. She gasped at the shock of it. He stopped and looked down at her with concern.

"Don't stop! That feels so damn good."

"I'm not going to stop. Remember I said you were going to come even if I had to fuck you all night. I'm prepared to stick with you until you do."

She believed him. Only she could already tell it wasn't going to take all night. It wouldn't even take ten minutes. Her climax crept up on her in steady steps. It seemed to rise with each kiss of his cock against her cervix. The pleasure-pain seduced her into compliance, and she shot over the top without warning, dragging Lamar with her by the sounds of the *fuck* ripped from his mouth.

Despite her utter exhaustion, she had to smile when he cursed again as he slowly pulled out of her pussy. He climbed off the bed after kissing the inside of her thigh and disappeared from sight. A few minutes later she heard the flush of the toilet and water running in the sink. It was the last thing she heard before she fell into an exhausted sleep.

* * * *

"She's out like a light." Brody yawned. He wasn't far behind.

"Think she's going to have regrets in the morning and try to push us away?"

"I don't know. That's what's so exciting about her. You never know what to expect from her."

"She already feels like a part of me, Brody. I don't want her to leave Riverbend. We've got to convince her to at least stay and work here even if we don't win her over right away. At least then we would have a chance."

"Yeah, if she goes to Austin, we'll have a much more difficult time convincing her. Plus, we'll have competition there. No way a beautiful woman like Caitlyn will go unnoticed in a place like Austin."

"We need some help with this. Who all do you know that takes their bookkeeping needs out of town?"

Brody rubbed a hand over his face. "I honestly don't know offhand, but we can check around. If we come up with several names, she'll have to really think about it."

"I wonder how many names she needs?" Lamar mused.

"Could ask her. I don't think that would hurt."

"I'll see if I can bring it up in conversation tomorrow. Then we can get to work getting the information we need."

"That's a plan then. In the meantime, let's try not to push too much and let her relax. She's going to be here for two weeks, maybe three. That should give us plenty of time to convince her that she belongs here in Riverbend."

"I think we have all our bases covered."

"Just as soon as you think that, something comes up to put a monkey wrench in your plans. Be careful what you say around her. I don't want to upset her and risk her running out early." Besides putting them in a bad situation with Brian, it would possibly ruin their chances at courting Caitlyn.

"I can't wait till she sees our books tomorrow. Maybe that alone will convince her to stay out of mercy for us." Brody smiled tiredly.

She had worn him out. God, she was amazing. He couldn't stop thinking about how she looked when she came with Lamar. It had surprised her. The shocked look had been priceless. He wanted to see many more of those expressions on her face over the coming years, preferably in their bed.

"What are the odds she'll come around, Brody?"

"I honestly don't know."

"I just don't think I can stand it if we lose her. If she backs off too far or for too long, I'm going to seduce her until she agrees."

Brody chuckled quietly. "Somehow I don't think that will work any better. Don't give up hope before we've even gotten started. We made progress tonight. She trusts us enough to let us in bed with her. That's a big step."

"Yeah, I know. I just hope it's a step in the right direction. You know how women can be. I don't want to end up the bad guy in her eyes. I want to see nothing but love there."

Chapter Nine

Caitlyn awoke in phases. At first, she thought she was dreaming. Then she realized she wasn't and she was lying between Brody and Lamar with a hand from each of them on her body. Brody's was on her stomach and Lamar's was on her breast. Confusion clouded her mind for a few seconds, and then it all came back to her in a rush.

She groaned and looked up at the ceiling. What was she going to do now? There was no going back with them. Of that she was sure. They would see having sex with them as a step toward a relationship.

Well, isn't it? You don't do casual sex, Caitlyn. What did you expect when you let them take you to bed?

She couldn't claim alcohol as the culprit. Certainly she'd been out of her head when she'd succumbed to their seduction, but even that was weak. No, she'd known what she had been doing. *Damn.*

She sighed. Not only had she had sex with them, but she'd slept in their bed all night. What would Brian say? Why hadn't he called looking for her? She frowned. He would think of it as a positive thing, a step toward having her move to Riverbend. Did he approve of Brian and Lamar as suitable men for her?

The idea that Brian would pair her up with them on purpose took root in her mind. She frowned at the thought.

"What's the frown for, baby?" Lamar's still-drowsy eyes were focused on her when she turned her head.

"I've been kidnapped and my brother hasn't even bothered to call looking for me."

Lamar laughed causing Brody to wake up enough to roll over and wrap his hand around her waist. She frowned deeper at this.

"We haven't kidnapped you and Brian knows you're a big girl. You can spend the night with us without his worrying."

"How does he know that something didn't happen to me?"

"Because we would have called him if something had happened. Nothing happened though. You're safe and sexy as hell first thing in the morning." He winced. "Well, except for that frown."

"I need to get up and get dressed so I can leave." She attempted to move Brody's heavy arm.

All she succeeded in doing was causing him to tighten his grip. He snuggled closer to her and buried his nose in her neck.

"Stop that, Brody." She squinched up her neck in protest. His cold nose poked her warm neck, making her squeal in protest.

"Ow, that was my ear you yelled in."

"That's my body you're holding down. I need to get up."

"Not until you promise to stay for breakfast. I'll cook scrambled eggs, toast, and bacon. How does that sound?"

"I really shouldn't stay any longer."

"It's already eight o'clock. No need to be in a hurry now."

"Don't you have to open the shop? Won't people be wondering where you are?"

"If they need us badly enough, they'll call. We don't have anything on deadline right now."

Lamar rolled out of bed and headed for the bathroom. Caitlyn used that opening to slide out of Brody's lax embrace to sit on the edge of the bed. She had to gather her wits about her. First things first. She needed to dress. She really needed a shower, but Lamar was probably already in the shower.

"Can I use the shower down the hall?"

"Of course, but Lamar would probably love for you to join him." Brody had rolled over to his side of the bed and sat up.

"I'll just use the other one." Showering with Lamar would be an utter disaster.

She could already imagine some of the things they might do in the shower. She had to shake her head to get the images out of her mind. Leave it to her to conjure up the very thing she was trying to avoid.

She picked up her clothes, realizing that her blouse was somewhere in the living room downstairs. She'd have to deal with that after her shower. After all, they had seen her nude already. She would have her bra on.

All during her shower, she fought the images of the three of them from the night before. Then she cringed at the smug look Brian would probably give her. He hadn't been the least surprised when she had told him that she was going out with Lamar and Brody. No doubt they had worked it out beforehand. The more she thought about it the madder she got at all of them.

She dressed after drying off, forgoing her panties, stuffing them in her pocket instead. She wasted a little time trying to tame her hair then sighed and walked out of the bathroom to find Lamar there holding out her blouse.

"Thought you would want this."

"Um, thanks." She looked into his eyes and saw worry and maybe just a little bit of fear. It diffused her anger at him.

She realized that she couldn't stay mad when they had been so attentive to her. She couldn't fault them in anything they had done while she had been with them. Brody was a bit demanding by nature, but so far he had curbed it for her benefit. She was sure that bossy bone was still there, but the fact that he was making an effort went a long way toward appeasing her aggravation with him.

"Brody is cooking breakfast. Are you about ready to go down?"

"Let me get my blouse on and I'll be right down." She stepped back into the bathroom and closed the door.

She guessed it was silly for her to do that when she had been standing right there in front of Lamar without it, but she felt better for having the privacy. Once again she looked in the mirror and pronounced herself as ready as she was going to get considering she'd spent the night and didn't have her things with her.

As she walked downstairs she tried to decide if she had known deep down inside that she was going to spend the night with them to begin with. Maybe it had been in the back of her mind that it was a possibility, yet the stubborn side of her refused to admit it. She didn't sleep around. Well, she hadn't before now.

"Morning, Caitydid. Are you hungry?" Brody stood at the stove dressed in well-fitting jeans and a T-shirt stretched tight across his broad shoulders.

"I figured I would just have some coffee and get one of you to take me back to Brian's."

"Nope. You're going to eat a healthy breakfast first. Then we'll take you back."

"Here's your coffee. Do you take anything in it?" Lamar handed her a cup.

"No, thanks. I drink it black."

Once again the bossy bone was in full view. At least he'd smiled when he'd said it, and he had gone to the trouble of cooking for her. The least *she* could do was eat it. Shrugging her shoulders so as not to appear that she'd given in so easily, Caitlyn sat at the bar and accepted the plate of eggs, bacon, and toast he handed her. She had to admit that it smelled good. When her stomach rumbled, she ducked her head.

The men both chuckled as they dug into their plates piled high with food. She guessed they burned a lot of calories doing what they did with welding and working with heavy materials.

As soon as they she finished, Caitlyn took her dishes to the sink and rinsed them off. She hesitated at loading them in the dishwasher. She didn't know if they used it or not. Some men didn't bother with it.

"Just set your plate by the sink. We'll tend to them later." Lamar came to her rescue.

She sat back down and waited for the men to finish eating. They each rinsed off their plates and set them on top of hers. Then Brody walked over to her and wrapped his arms around her before she realized what he was going to do. He looked down in her face and smiled.

"Last night was beautiful. Don't overthink it, Caitlyn. We're all adults, and you mean a lot to us." He hugged her and kissed the top of her head.

Then he passed her off to Lamar who hugged her as well and kissed her forehead before letting her go.

"Ready to leave?" Brody pulled out his keys.

"Um, yeah. I better go if I'm going to get back here by one to work on your books."

She almost missed their look of relief when she said that. They had obviously thought she might back out of helping them work on their books. She wasn't going to be petty and refuse to help them with something like that. She was better than that. It hurt her that they had believed the worst.

Brody led the way out to the truck. He climbed up in the driver's seat, and Lamar helped her up on the passenger's side, getting in beside her. He draped his arm behind her along the back of the seat. She expected him to let it fall to her shoulders on the ride down to Brian's house, but he didn't.

It only took five minutes to reach her brother's place, but it was a long five minutes to her. She kept expecting them to say something. Maybe they thought she should say something. What did she say? This was all new to her.

When they pulled up into the drive, Brody surprised her by turning off the engine and getting out of the cab. Lamar helped her down and the two men walked her to the door. She knocked, much to their amusement.

"What?"

"I wouldn't think you would need to knock. You're Brian's sister and are staying with him," Brody said.

Before she could answer him, Andy opened the door.

"Hey, you don't have to knock. Come on in." He backed up and held the door until all three of them had entered. "Brian is already at the store with Tish. I'm running late."

"Oh. Okay."

Somehow the fact that Brian hadn't stayed at home waiting on her to be sure she was okay bothered her. The fact that she'd been dreading it and had worked herself up into telling him to mind his own business didn't sit well with her. How could she be angry with him when she was a grown woman and didn't need his approval? She had just had words with him for butting into her business, so how could she be angry with him for *not* being there, butting into her business?

She huffed out a breath and relegated herself to sucking it up and admitting that she wanted his involvement in some things. She wasn't sure how she expected him to know which things.

"I'll just change clothes and head over there." She turned to Lamar and Brody, unsure of what to say to them.

"Thanks for bringing me home."

They grinned knowing smiles and nodded. Then they each gave her a brief kiss before nodding at Andy and leaving.

"I'll wait on you so you don't have to take your car."

"Thanks, but I need it today. I'm going back to their house at one to work on their books some."

"Okay. I'll be leaving in a few minutes. Just lock up behind you." Andy smiled and disappeared into what she knew was the office.

Caitlyn hurried up the stairs to her room and changed clothes. She spent a few minutes in the bathroom brushing her teeth and combing her hair to make herself presentable. Then she hurried downstairs. She locked the house behind her and headed to town. When she arrived at the store, Andy was just getting out of his truck. He smiled and waved as she pulled in.

When she walked into the store, Brian greeted her with a smile. He didn't look worried, upset, or smug. She felt her earlier ire deflate. If he was going to act as if there was nothing out of the ordinary, then so would she.

"Sorry I'm late."

"No problem. It's not like you work for me or anything. Besides, you have most everything taken care of. In fact, we're going to finish up early today and cut out after lunch. Tomorrow is the wedding rehearsal and Tish has things to do to get ready."

"Should I take her out tomorrow night? I haven't even thought about a bachelorette party. I'm not a good sister." She realized she had been so wrapped up in her own problems that she hadn't thought about what she should do as the sister to the groom.

"You're a great sister. We're not having the traditional night-before parties. We're going to have a nice quiet dinner and an early night instead. We have two ceremonies to get through on Saturday."

"Oh, that's nice. I'll make myself scarce tomorrow night. I'll rent a hotel room for the night."

"Don't be crazy. You're invited. You're my sister." Brian frowned.

"I don't want to be in the way, Brian. This is your time. Yours, Andy's, and Tish's."

"Doesn't matter. We're all family."

She let it go, determined to do something. She'd figure it out before tomorrow night. In the meantime, she needed to help Tish finish up the mail-order business side. She found the other woman in the back scratching her head.

"What is it?" Caitlyn asked.

"Oh, hi, Caitlyn. I was just trying to figure out where this invoice went on the books. It's for gifts for helping with the store when we were setting up. They wouldn't take payment. Most of the people here volunteer their services when a new business sets up in town." She waved the invoice in the air.

"Put it under miscellaneous. I didn't set up anything for gifts. I suppose we should do that. You will probably send out more gifts around Christmas. Hold up and let me work on that." She sat down and lost herself in the world of accounting.

When she finally looked up again it was to find that it was nearly twelve. Tish walked in about that time with Brian and Andy right behind her.

"Time to go, Caitlyn." She smiled. "Oh, and we've got an appointment at the spa tomorrow afternoon."

"We do?" It was the first she had heard about that. "I didn't even know there was a spa in town."

"I made appointments for us and my maid of honor for tomorrow at one. We're getting the works. We're going shopping. I'd invite you, but Andy said you already have plans." Tish smiled a wide smile, which was mirrored by Brian.

It was obvious they approved of her helping Brody and Lamar with their books. She wasn't sure how she felt about that. They were blatantly matchmaking it seemed. If she wasn't sure before, she was sure now. Part of her was amused and part of her was a little miffed that they thought she needed help. Never mind that she'd made a mess of her personal life so far. Thoughts of her false marriage irritated her. She worked to put it out of her mind.

She shrugged. "I promised Brody and Lamar I would take a look at their books to give them some help while I'm here. It's nothing major."

"It's really nice of you to help them. They are great guys and from the sounds of it, theirs are in a lot worse shape than ours were," Tish said.

"I don't know how much help I can be in such a short time, but I'll do what I can."

She walked out with them and was surprised to see Lamar driving up in the truck. She gave him a puzzled look and walked over to where he had parked behind her SUV.

"Hey. What's up?" She watched him climb out of the truck.

"I came to take you to lunch. Brody would have come, but he's meeting with a client."

"Oh. I was going to eat with them." She turned and noticed that the others had piled into Brian's truck and were backing out of the parking space.

"Looks like they assumed you were going with me anyway."

She frowned at the others when they waved at her. Had they already known Lamar was coming or did they just assume that since he was there he planned to take her to lunch? She seriously needed to talk to Brian about his making assumptions where she was concerned. She couldn't believe that he was so desperate to have her live in Riverbend that he would foist her off on two men she barely knew.

Didn't stop you from sleeping with them.

She realized that she hadn't moved, and Lamar was staring at her expectantly. Should she refuse and find something to eat at Brian's or give up and go along with him? Maybe making a stand here and now would be a good idea. Then maybe, doing it without Brody there wasn't fair. She bit her lower lip and sighed.

"Sure. Lunch sounds good."

He smiled and escorted her around to the passenger side of the truck to help her in. Once he was back inside the cab, he backed out of the parking place and headed toward the diner. She half expected to see Brian and the others there. She supposed they might have decided to go home to eat. Or they drove to Austin to shop and planned a late lunch, early dinner.

"What are you thinking so hard about?" Lamar escorted her to a table.

"Just wondering where the others decided to eat. They were going shopping afterward."

"Would you have rather gone with them?"

"No, I had already planned to work on your books. I'm not much of a shopper anyway."

"A woman who doesn't shop? I can't believe there is such an animal."

"Smart-ass." She couldn't help but grin at him.

The same young waitress from the first night she'd driven into town took their order. She smiled and winked at Caitlyn. No doubt she figured she was hooking up with Lamar. Then again, she sort of had.

They both ordered hamburgers and fries and talked about the upcoming marriage on Saturday.

"If they are going to have the normal intimate dinner on Friday night, why don't you come over and stay with Brody and I? We'll grill out and watch a movie."

"I'm not sure that's such a good idea."

"Why not?"

"You know why not," she whispered.

Caitlyn didn't want to discuss it in public. She hoped Lamar would pick up on that and leave it alone. To her relief, he changed the subject to the state of their books and they stayed on the subject until he signaled for the check.

"Are you expecting Brody to make it to go over the books with us?" She noticed that his truck wasn't at the house when they drove up.

"He said as soon as they finished going over the client's plans he would come home."

"Good, we all need to work on them together. Both of you seem to have worked on them at some point so it's safe to say that you'll continue sharing the duties."

"Yeah, it always depends on which one of us has the time when it needs doing. Of course we both put it off as long as we can, which is why it's in such bad shape." He grinned at her as they walked into the house.

"You don't look a bit guilty about it either."

"Hey, I work in a machine shop. I don't know the first thing about bookkeeping."

"If you would work on them on a routine basis, you wouldn't have to spend so much time on them when you do work on them. Plus, they would be in much better shape."

She followed him into the office and sighed at the multiple piles of papers waiting for her to organize. She started to walk around the desk and get to work, but Lamar pulled her into his arms and kissed her. Just like that, her pussy grew wet as her body applauded his bold move. Instead of pushing him away, she found herself drawing him closer. When he slowly pulled away, she realized she was clinging to him like grapevine on an arbor. Heat poured over her as embarrassment for her actions sent her blood pressure even higher. What was happening to her that she couldn't control herself around the two men? Even now, she wanted to clear off the desk and ride Lamar like a horse at the Kentucky Derby. Lust was going to be the death of her.

Chapter Ten

"I'm sorry. I—I don't know what's happening to me. I don't usually jump on men I hardly know. I don't go to bed with men I don't know." She realized she was shaking all over and backed away from him.

"Easy, Caitlyn. It's all right. You do know us and I know you're not someone who normally does things like that. We're attracted to each other on a deeper level than just sex."

She felt tears stinging behind her eyes and blinked to keep them from falling. What was going on with her? She wasn't usually so emotional either. Even when Harold had told her about his real wife she hadn't gotten overemotional.

"I don't know what to think." She walked around the desk, putting it between them.

He didn't try to follow her or force her to admit to anything. He just stood there looking wounded. She hated that she had put that look on his face but couldn't think of anything that would wipe it away, either.

"Let's just start working on the books. You can catch Brody up once he gets here. I'm sure it won't be much longer."

"That sounds like a good idea." She eased into the soft leather desk chair and waited while Lamar drew up another chair.

They worked together with Lamar explaining what the invoices and various papers were. By the time Brody arrived, she had a small semblance of an idea on how the business worked. It was a basic supply-and-demand manufacturing business. They made things and sold them. Nearly ninety percent of the business was for items ordered ahead of time to be made and then delivered. They had some standard items that they kept made up because they were always making them for someone, and they wore out so easily.

"You started without me." Brody teased.

"Don't worry, there's plenty for you to do." She patted the other side of the desk where several piles of paper still stood. "Pull up a chair and let me go over how everything works."

"I'd rather have a kiss first." He bent over the chair and caught her chin in his big hand.

"W–wait." She tried to push back in the chair, but he was holding it still.

"Nope. You're not going to get away with cheating me out of my kiss. I'm sure Lamar got his."

Lamar's soft snort *and then some,* wasn't lost on her. She glared at him. He had the grace to look guilty.

When Brody leaned down, she found herself turning her face up to meet his mouth. She couldn't deny her attraction to them any longer. She was obviously susceptible to their charms. It was the only thing she could think of that made sense. Not only were they serious eye candy, but they had manners and were up front about what they wanted from her. It was what they wanted that had her spooked. She wasn't looking for anything long lasting. She had to get on with her life, and they were proving to be a tasty but dangerous roadblock.

When Brody's lips met hers, she sighed into them. She hadn't realized she'd been waiting for that moment ever since Lamar's simple kiss had turned into a firestorm of sensation. Electricity burned between them as he cupped the back of her head to hold it steady while he explored her open mouth. His tongue slid alongside hers before licking along the roof and outer walls. She moaned when he would have pulled away. Instead, he deepened the kiss, pulling her out of the chair into his arms.

Caitlyn had to admit that she went willingly. She wanted that kiss as much as she wanted her next breath. She didn't even balk when

Lamar plastered himself against her back, making it plain by the hardness of his cock that he wanted her. Without second-guessing herself, she wrapped both arms around Brody but pulled away from the kiss.

"Please. I need you. Both of you." She waited while Brody searched her eyes.

"What about the books?" he asked with a small smile.

"They'll still be here later."

Lamar pressed his rock-hard dick against the small of her back. She rolled her eyes as her panties grew even damper than they were before. All it seemed to take was their kiss or a touch and she was putty in their hands.

Brody picked her up and carried her through the house to the stairs. He didn't hesitate there in the least. Her confidence in his being able to carry her up them had grown. She looked over his shoulder to where Lamar was following them. His face had stiffened into pure need.

Brody let her slide down his body until she was standing on her feet. She was glad he didn't let her go since she wasn't sure she could stand on her own. Her legs felt like jelly as the two men began undressing her. She had a silly thought that at least all her clothes would be upstairs when she got ready to dress again.

"It's my turn to taste her sweet honey." Lamar undressed in mere seconds.

Brody took his time, drawing her eyes to his hands as he removed each item of clothing. When his hardened cock leapt free of his briefs, she had to swallow at the sight.

Then Lamar was pressing her back toward the bed. He seemed to have a one-track mind that was focused on her pussy. As soon as she was draped back over the covers, he dove between her legs to shoulder them wide. He didn't waste any time. He spread her pussy lips and curled his tongue up her slit like a man dying for water in the desert.

His brother lapped at her belly button and then moved up her abdomen to lick between her breasts. He left a wet trail with his mouth everywhere he went. He nipped and sucked what felt like every square inch of her skin from the waist up except for her breasts. Finally, she couldn't take it any longer and grabbed his head with both hands. She pulled him down to her breast with a growl. He chuckled but latched on to her nipple and sucked long and hard. She thought she would come from that alone.

"Oh, God, yes!" She couldn't help the words escaping her mouth as he pulled on her other nipple with his fingers.

Lamar had changed tactics and was sucking on her pussy lips now. He seemed intent on cleaning her of all of her cream. He licked over her clit several times, making her squirm. When he chuckled against her sex, she couldn't help the shudder that traveled down her spine. Once again he surprised her when he entered her cunt with two fingers, wiggling them around until he found her hot spot. His fingers pressed against it over and over with just enough pressure to light a fire in her blood.

With each stroke of his tongue across her clit and the light pressure of his fingers on her sweet spot, Caitlyn's climax grew inside of her. Even as she began to pant to keep breath in her lungs, Lamar was ramping up his attention to her clit.

Brody tormented her breasts with his fingers, teeth, and tongue. It seemed as if he wanted to make her come from that alone. The truth be told, she could, but with Lamar eating her alive with his fingers in her cunt, she was close to climaxing already.

Dear God!

Lamar sucked in her clit and pressed on it with his tongue as he stroked her sweet spot with his fingers. She began to quake all over as her climax welled up inside of her. She exploded when Brody bit lightly on one nipple and pinched the nipple of the other breast at the same time. She bucked beneath them as Lamar sucked up her cum and Brody continued to nip and pinch on her nipples. When she finally began to settle down again, Lamar suited up.

"Come on, baby. Turn over for me. I want to fuck that pretty pussy doggy style."

No one had ever talked to her the way he and Brody did. It was nasty, and it turned her on immensely. She turned over and got on her hands and knees. She looked over her shoulder as Lamar pressed his sheathed dick against her slit. When he began to press into her wet pussy, she moaned at the pressure against her swollen folds.

"Fuck, you're so damn tight, Caity. I'm not going to last long once I'm inside of you."

Slowly, he pushed in and out of her until he managed to lodge himself deep in her cunt. He stopped moving, hugging her hips to him for a few seconds. Then he started pumping his cock in and out of her in slow measured thrusts.

Caitlyn looked at Lamar's ruddy cock and licked her lips. She wondered if she could deep-throat all of that perfect male flesh. She looked up at him and opened her mouth. He didn't need an invitation. He slipped his engorged dick into her mouth. She ran her tongue all around it then sucked tightly on just the cockhead.

"Aw, hell, baby. That feels too fucking good."

She continued licking and sucking as she slowly bobbed her head up and down on his massive cock. He finally grabbed her head and held on as she slowly went deeper and deeper.

"Suck it, baby. Suck it all the way down."

She moaned around him and he curled his fingers into her scalp. She relaxed her throat and took him to the back and then swallowed around him.

"Yes! Just like that. Do it again, Caity."

She did it again then came off of him with a slight rasp of her teeth along his dick. He groaned and began fucking her mouth in short, even jabs. She reached up with one hand and fingered his balls before Lamar's thrusts began to get harder and she needed both hands to stay upright.

"I'm going to come, baby. Let me go."

She redoubled her efforts to suck him back down her throat, intent on swallowing his cum. She didn't want to waste a single drop. He groaned and began to jerk as his cock spurted ribbons of the salty, tangy liquid down her throat. She fought to keep up with it and breathe at the same time.

"Fuck!" Brody collapsed back against the headboard as his softening cock spilled from her mouth.

Caitlyn couldn't believe how close she was to coming again. Between swallowing Brody's cum and Lamar pounding into her pussy and rasping over her G-spot with nearly every stroke, she was so close to flying that she could almost touch it. She couldn't help squeezing down on Lamar's thick dick as she began to meet his thrusts with some of her own. They pounded into each other until her climax poured over her in a warm rush that filled her entire body with burning heat. She was sure her skin burned a rosy red all over.

Lamar began to rotate his hips as he shuttled his cock in and out of her. The slight movement prolonged her climax to the point of pain, but it was a delicious sort of pain. One she didn't mind one bit. Then he was shouting her name and pouring his cum into the condom. She could feel the heat of it against her cunt as he filled the rubber. He leaned over her panting in her ear as he fought to breathe as well.

"Your pussy nearly sucked my fucking dick off."

She smiled but couldn't say anything yet. Her arms gave way under Lamar's weight, and she turned her head just in time to keep from burying her face in the covers.

"Get off of her, Lamar. You're going to suffocate her." Brody's chuckle made it obvious that he wasn't seriously fussing at his brother.

Lamar got back up and carefully backed off her. As if his cock was the only thing holding her up, Caitlyn fell to the bed in a heap with her ass still in the air. She was sure she didn't look very ladylike, but in that instant, she didn't care. All that mattered right then was catching her breath and relaxing her muscles. They were still strung tight from her shuddering climax.

Brody pulled her body up the bed until she was lying prone with her head on his shoulder. He ran a finger up and down her arm. When Lamar came back to bed, he released his possessive hold on her and let his brother wrap a leg over hers. They both seemed to want to touch her.

"Caitlyn, what happened with your marriage?" Brody asked after a few minutes of silence.

She froze. What did she tell them? Somehow the truth seemed too much like a reality TV show. Still, it wasn't in her to outright lie. She must have been quiet too long, because he tilted her head up so that he could look into her eyes.

"Nothing you can tell us will change how we feel about you, Caity. It's okay."

"I'm not sure where to begin. I married Harold thinking we were well suited for each other. I guess I thought it was love, but I figured out later that I didn't really love him. Still, for better or for worse, you know." She licked her lips and continued.

"Anyway, he was a medical supply salesman and was on the road a lot. I never once thought he would cheat on me. He was devoted to me to a fault when he was home. We rarely argued over anything. We just seemed right together." She paused to gather her thoughts.

"Were you happy?" Lamar asked quietly.

"I thought I was. I realize now that I was fooling myself because I thought it was forever."

"What happened?" Brody squeezed her shoulder.

"Several years ago I was ready to start a family. Harold wanted to put it off another year or two. We argued about it for several months, but then he changed his mind and agreed. He said he was just worried that financially we weren't ready yet. I knew we were doing fine, so I didn't think anything of it."

Caitlyn thought back to that time and realized she should have suspected something was wrong by the about-face that he had pulled. He'd been too eager to get started, but she hadn't seen it. She had been too excited about the idea of having a baby.

"After several months of trying and I hadn't been able to get pregnant, I went to the doctor. He said that I had a tilted uterus but that with time I should be able to conceive. I was worried, but he had assured me that it was possible. We kept trying, but after another year, I felt like a failure, because I couldn't manage to get pregnant. I was devastated. Harold was supportive and understanding. He talked about adopting and said maybe I just needed to relax and not focus on trying so hard. I really thought he understood and cared that I was upset."

"Having a baby was important to you. Still, there are other ways. There's artificial insemination. Did he even suggest that?" Brody asked in a strained voice.

"No, and at the time, I wasn't thinking straight or I would have thought about it or gone back to the doctor and he probably would have gone over our options with us. A year later, I came home to find Harold there waiting on me. He looked different, worried. I thought at first he had lost his job when he told me he had something to tell me, that I needed to sit down. I felt my stomach drop to my toes. I knew it would be bad."

She drew in a deep breath knowing it would be easier to say if she just spit it out. Still, she hesitated. She realized then that what they thought about what she had to say mattered to her. Would they think she was stupid for having not suspected something?

"He told me that he was married to another woman in another city. He'd been married to her when he supposedly married me. He said he had fallen in love with me but loved her, too and couldn't give either of us up at the time. I never suspected that he was already married. Nothing pointed to it."

"The bastard!" Lamar rose up on his elbow and stared down into her eyes. "He used you, Caitlyn. You trusted him. Don't beat yourself up over not knowing."

"There's more. He hadn't planned on telling me ever, but his real wife found out he was *seeing* me and threatened to take away his son and daughter. Finding out that he had children with her hurt just as much as finding out that I had never been married to the bastard in the first place. I spent five years of my life living with him without being married. I just stared at him. I couldn't believe it. Then he told me the rest of his news. He'd had a vasectomy right after his daughter was born. It had never been my fault that I couldn't conceive at all. He let me think that for years." Tears formed in her eyes. She wiped them away.

Why it felt like only yesterday that she'd learned the news, Caitlyn didn't know. It felt fresh again, but somehow telling them lessened the sting this time.

"I hope you turned him in for bigamy. He deserves to go to jail." Brody had stiffened up all over.

"I couldn't do it. I thought about his kids and just couldn't do it to them. They would have ended up the ones to suffer for it in the long run. Plus, I just wanted to forget all about it. I wanted it to all just go away."

"Honey, you know that none of it was your fault, don't you?" Lamar wiped a tear from the corner of her eye.

"I can't help but think that I should have suspected that he was cheating on me at the very least. A woman should sense those things. Except for my inability to get pregnant, there had never been any stress between us. He didn't make secretive phone calls or go out late at night. He was gone a few nights a week, but he had hospitals that he visited all over the state."

"Stop it. You're not to blame and women don't always know. It doesn't mean you were to blame or that you deserved any of it." Brody pulled her farther onto him so that she was almost draped across his chest. "I don't want you to think about it anymore. It's in the past. This is now, and Lamar and I care about you and want a chance at proving to you that we are serious."

"Don't you see? I've just gotten out of a bad situation. I can't think about getting into anything serious right now. It's too soon." She slid off of him and sat up.

"It's too late, Caity. You already are. We're serious about you, serious about a relationship with you, and I'm not giving up," Lamar said.

Chapter Eleven

Both men sat up next to her. They didn't try to touch her. For that she was grateful. She needed some distance while she calmed back down. Only Lamar's words were far from soothing to her already troubled mind.

"I should go." She started to scoot to the bottom of the bed to get out.

Brody stopped her by wrapping an arm around her waist. "Whoa. You're not going anywhere 'til we finish talking."

"We are finished. I knew better than to get involved, but I did it anyway. I mean, what's one more affair. I just came off of a five-year one."

"Stop it right now, Caitlyn. I'm not going to let you belittle yourself. You had no idea what was going on. That's final." He turned to Lamar. "Go run a bath, Lamar. She needs something to help her relax."

Lamar nodded and slipped off the bed to pad quickly toward the bathroom. Brody pulled her closer to him, burying his face in her hair.

"A bath isn't going to change my mind, Brody. I need to go before we all do something that makes it even harder."

"Makes what harder?"

"My leaving when the time comes. I'm moving to Austin, Brody. I've already told you that I'm not going to live this close to Brian. I love him, but we would drive each other crazy."

"We aren't asking for forever right now, Caitlyn. All we're asking for is a chance to get to know you and show you how serious we are. I know you can't see it right now, but we belong together."

"See, that's what I'm talking about. You're talking forever or something, and I can't give you that."

"Just forget about forever and concentrate on the here and the now."

"What about me? Don't you think that it's going to hurt me to get more involved with you and then leave in a few weeks?"

"So you'll throw away the possibility of something wonderful because you're scared you'll get hurt?"

"Hurt again, Brody. It's too soon for me. Can't you understand that?"

Lamar walked back into the bedroom. He looked from her to Brody and back again.

"I've got the bath ready, Caity. Come on. You'll feel better after you've relaxed for a while."

She closed her eyes for a few seconds, and then scooted off the bed when Brody released her. She followed Lamar to the bathroom and let him help her slip into the welcoming water. The tub was big enough for three, but only Lamar got in with her. Brody didn't even come into the bathroom.

Lamar pulled her into his arms. She leaned back against him, using his chest as a pillow. He didn't say anything at first, but after a few minutes, he began to talk.

"Brody and I have been looking for someone to share our life with for a long time. He had about given up on finding anyone but kept looking for my sake. I refused to give up. I could tell that he had lost hope, though. Then you ran into that ditch and I saw interest in his eyes for the first time."

"Lamar..."

"Wait, Caitlyn. He cares about you more than I would have believed so soon after meeting you. I knew almost immediately that you were the one for us. I know you're not ready for anything long term yet. I get that. He will, too. Just give him time. When the time comes for you to leave, we'll drive to Austin and see you as often as we can. Just give us the chance to court you. Eventually, one day you'll be ready for more."

She mulled his words over in her head. Could she do that, date them for a while and see where it took them? Was her heart strong enough not to succumb to their charm and charisma? If she fell for them and it didn't work out, it would break her heart. She didn't think she could stand much more heartbreak.

Caitlyn sighed and tried to measure her words. She wasn't sure if she was making the right decision, but she'd already come this far with them. She admitted to herself that if they stopped seeing each other now, she'd still be hurt. She was already emotionally invested in them even after only a few days. She didn't know how it had happened, but it had.

"I can't promise you forever, Lamar, but I will give you a chance. It's the best I can do. If you're still interested by the time I move, then we can talk about dating."

Lamar squeezed her. "That's all we're asking."

They soaked there for several more minutes until the water began to cool. Then Lamar helped her out and dried her off. They walked into the bedroom to find it empty. Brody was gone. She wondered if he had left the house entirely or if he was downstairs. Somehow the idea that he'd walked out bothered her. If she were honest, she'd admit that it hurt.

They dressed with Lamar hindering her more than helping her. She had to smile at his playful nature. He and Brody were the exact opposites. Where Lamar was lighthearted and relaxed, Brody was stiff and serious. The fact that she had seen him relaxed and in a playful mood reiterated that he was serious about her. She was sure he didn't let down his guard with many people.

When they got downstairs, she was disappointed not to see him waiting on them. Lamar didn't seem worried. He led her back to the office and there he was, going over what she'd already accomplished. He looked up when they walked into the room.

He shot a glance at Lamar and seemed to lose some of his stiffness. She guessed that Lamar had somehow reassured him.

"You've managed to get a lot done in just a little while."

"Not really. All I did was start to organize everything. I still need to try to get your books set up on the computer so you can enter them directly into the program and stop trying to use books and journals. It will be easier on you in the long run because the computer can sum everything for you. It will also give you reports to let you know how you're doing financially."

"It sounds complicated," Lamar said.

"It's not. I'll show you, but I've got to get back to work. I won't have much time to work on them."

"What about tomorrow? I know that Brian and them aren't planning on going in to work the store." Brody watched her face.

"Um, I'm supposed to go with Tish and her maid of honor to the spa tomorrow morning. Um, after that I suppose I could work on them."

"You'll enjoy that," Lamar said.

"Afterward will be good. Why don't you bring some things over with you to stay the night?" Brody didn't look at her this time.

"Don't forget they have dinner tomorrow night at the house."

"I guess that would be a good idea. I had planned to stay at a hotel for the night."

"There's no need for that. Stay with us. You can work on the books while you're here." Brody gave a half smile.

"We can all go to the ceremonies together." Lamar grinned as well.

She knew she was going to cave. All it really took was the little half smile on Brody's face to convince her.

"Okay. I'll stay with you guys. It's probably the only way Brian will be satisfied with me not eating with them tomorrow night. I don't want to be in the way."

"We'll go pick up your clothes in a little while. Don't forget you need to bring your dress for the ceremony as well." Lamar squeezed her shoulder.

"Move out of the way, Brody. I need to get back to work." Caitlyn shook her head and walked around the desk to push him out of the way.

He vacated the desk chair without a fuss. They positioned themselves on either side of her to watch what she was doing. They worked like that until five that afternoon. Brody finally called a halt to it, reminding them they needed to go get Caitlyn's clothes.

"I wonder if they will be home yet." She had a key to the house but hoped the others would be around. She needed to tell Brian what she planned to do.

They arrived at her brother's house only to find that they hadn't returned yet. She used her key and hurried to her room to pack a few things in the overnight case. She carried it and her dress downstairs. Lamar immediately took both from her.

"I'll go put this in the truck. Do you want to call him and tell him you're staying with us or leave a note?"

She grimaced. She supposed leaving a note would be the cowardly thing to do. She should call him. By the time Lamar had returned, she had made up her mind to call. Brody had been quietly waiting on her to make up her mind. Now he smiled at her, nodding his approval. That made her feel good, much to her chagrin.

She walked into the kitchen and pressed speed dial on her cell phone and waited for him to answer.

"Hey, sis. What's up?"

"Hey, um, you don't have to worry about me tomorrow night. I'm going to stay with Brody and Lamar until after the wedding. I'll go with Tish Friday morning and then come back here to work on their books. We'll go to the weddings together."

"I'm glad you three are getting along so well. They're good men. You're still invited to dinner tomorrow. You're family, Caitlyn."

"Thanks, Brian, but I'm going to let you three do your thing. I would only put a damper on the, um, festivities."

"You're sure you'll be okay there?"

"Yeah, I'll be fine. Don't worry about me. Just enjoy yourself."

They said goodbye and Caitlyn hit *end* on the phone. She shoved it back in her pocket. There was no going back now. She hoped she had made the right decision. She had already decided that her heart was in more danger than she had thought. She would need to shore up her defenses to be sure she didn't lose her heart.

"Ready to go now?" Lamar interrupted her thoughts.

She smiled and nodded. They locked up the house and drove back down to their house. She wasn't sure how to act now that they were back. It was all still new to her, this relationship that they insisted they had with her.

"I'm going to fix dinner. Why don't you and Brody relax and watch TV while I put something together?"

"I'll help," she said.

"No need. I already know what I want to cook. I'll have it ready in no time." Lamar shook his head.

"Come on. Lamar doesn't like anyone in the kitchen when he's cooking." Brody took her hand and pulled her toward the couch.

They sat down and Brody grabbed the remote. He flipped through channels until he found something to watch. She only half listened as she mulled over what she had agreed to. After a little while, Brody interrupted her thoughts.

"You're not watching TV, Caity. What are you thinking so hard about?"

She hesitated in telling him, but decided he needed to know that she still wasn't comfortable with getting so involved with them.

"I'm worried that someone is going to get hurt. Long-distance relationships rarely if ever work."

"It will be okay. You'll see. Now don't think about it anymore. I don't want you stressing over it. Let us doing the worrying if any worrying is going to happen." He squeezed her around the shoulders and kissed her cheek before settling back into the TV show.

Before long, Lamar announced dinner was ready. They sat down at the bar and ate with Brody filling Lamar in on the client he'd been meeting with earlier that day. Caitlyn didn't understand most of what they were talking about. She did recognize the bookkeeping opportunities in what he was saying. She refrained from pointing them out until he had finished.

"Did you write up an estimate or even a ticket for his order?" she asked.

"No, around here we pretty much shake on a quote. There isn't any record of it anywhere."

"The quote would go a long way in helping you keep up with not only what you have due to complete, but also strengthen your claim as a small business. The government is just looking for an excuse to deny your income tax claims."

"I never thought about it that way. I guess I need to start writing them up. I don't have to give them to the customer. I can just keep them for proof and it would probably help me when I'm ordering supplies."

"That's right. You can keep up with inventory that way. I can set up an inventory list for you. It should help you be more efficient."

Lamar spoke up. "It sure would be nice to know where we stand on our supplies. I hate running out of something in the middle of a project."

"I'm glad I can help you. Lamar, we're going to have to set up a time next week when I can review the bookkeeping process with you since you're the one who primarily works with them."

"That sounds fine. I can pretty much meet you here anytime you want. We'll be around the store a good bit to help you with the mail-order business." Lamar smiled.

She frowned. "I told you I could handle it."

"We're just going to help with the larger packages. They'll be awkward, and you don't need to be lifting things you don't have to." Brody's expression was serious.

"Fine. You can handle the big things." She guessed she could let them do that.

She still wasn't sure about spending so much time with them when she was going to leave as soon as she'd shown Tish the books. For some reason, that didn't sound as inviting as it had before. She had been looking forward to the relocation to Austin. Now, the thought of leaving them just didn't feel right. She hoped she wasn't doing something that would only hurt them all in the long run, something like falling in love.

Chapter Twelve

Caitlyn woke early the next morning to Brody wrapped around her like a hungry python. She was glad she could breathe. She turned her head and noticed that Lamar was turned on his side facing away from her. She hoped he wasn't miffed that Brody had effectively hogged her.

"Morning." Brody's husky voice greeted her.

"Morning. Think you could let me up? I need to get to the bathroom."

Brody chuckled and slowly unwound himself from around her. She quickly climbed over him and off the bed. She hurried to the bathroom before she embarrassed herself. She went ahead and freshened up, using her things she'd brought from Brian's place. Tomorrow was the big day for them. She prayed that they were doing the right thing and Brian wasn't making a terrible mistake.

She walked out of the bathroom to find Lamar missing and Brody getting dressed. She put away her nightclothes and gathered up her things. She wasn't going to go back to Brian's house that night, so she was glad she had picked up several outfits in addition to her dress for the wedding.

"Lamar is fixing breakfast. We have to go in to work today. You can work on the books if you want to or just laze around the house until time for your spa treatment with Tish."

Caitlyn bristled at first at his telling her what she could do with her morning. Then she sighed and reminded herself that it was just how Brody talked. He didn't mean anything about it. She would have to get used to his bossy ways if they were going to date. Normally, she could get along with anyone, but with it being someone she was planning on dating, it was a little more difficult.

"What?" Brody asked staring at her.

"Nothing."

"No, it's something. What?"

Caitlyn shook her head. "You're bossy, Brody. Try not to tell me what to do."

"Oh, I wasn't. If I wanted to be bossy, I would tell you that you couldn't go anywhere while we were gone. See, that's bossy."

She rolled her eyes and shook her head. Then she turned on her heel and walked through the door and down the stairs. Just as she reached the bottom, he grabbed her from behind and turned her around and kissed her. He worked slow and deep, as if his tongue was slowly memorizing every nook and cranny of her mouth. She moaned into his as he sucked on her mouth.

When he released her, she swayed in his arms. Yep, he totally rocked her world with that kiss. She doubted she would be coherent for at least the next fifteen minutes. Sure enough, when she entered the kitchen, she couldn't think what to say to Lamar. She just stared at him. He grinned as if knowing what was wrong with her, and maybe he did. He looked smug. She narrowed her eyes at him but didn't say anything.

"Have a seat, you guys, breakfast is served."

They ate in relative silence with one of the guys speaking around mouthfuls of waffle or bacon. It was delicious, but that word couldn't do the meal justice. Once she had finished, she rinsed off her plate and sat back down with a second cup of coffee. She wasn't sure what she was going to do with her morning but figured she would work on their books. The sooner she got them done, the sooner she could teach Lamar what to do. Then she could leave for Austin with a clear conscience.

The men's stools scraped back from the bar as they gathered their plates to rinse them and put them in the dishwasher. Brody kissed her goodbye. Lamar drew her in for a hug and a kiss. She couldn't help but kiss him back.

"We'll be home by the time you're finished with your spa treatment. Have fun, Caity." Brody led the way outside to the truck.

Alone, she sat at the island enjoying her coffee and thinking about her life. She had so many decisions to make over the next two weeks. She had to admit that she still wasn't one hundred percent sure about anything at this point. Starting her own business sounded like a dream come true, but could she make a go of it? And what about Brian? How much of his nosey ways could she take?

She rinsed out her coffee cup and put it in the dishwasher then rinsed out the coffeepot and emptied the filter and grounds. Then she walked into the office and pulled on her accountant clothes like an armor and began the arduous task of sorting through their papers to get them ready for entering into the computer program.

The next time she looked up, it was nearly twelve. She panicked. She had to meet Tish at the spa. She had the directions but wasn't sure how long it would take to get to the place. She hurried and closed down the program before heading upstairs to freshen up before heading toward the spa.

Once she arrived, she had to admit the directions were easy to follow. The spa itself was decorated in pastel colors that were easy on the eyes and soothing. Gentle instrumental music played low in the background. The three women greeted each other, with Tish performing the introductions.

"Caitlyn, this is Rita. Rita, this is Caitlyn. She's Brian's sister."

Rita smiled. "It's a pleasure to meet you. I can't wait 'til they open their store. I've peeked in the window and see a lot of things I like."

"Thank you. I'm sure they would be glad to give you a private showing one day."

"That would be awesome."

They settled into their chairs and waited for their treatments. Tish and Rita kept up a steady conversation about different people they knew and the town itself. Caitlyn learned a lot about the area and the people that lived there. For the most part, they were all friendly, she realized.

"How do you like Riverbend so far, Caitlyn?" Rita's words were stilted since she was in the middle of a facial and had something blue on her face.

"It seems like a very nice place to live. Everyone here has been wonderful."

"Tish tells me you're an accountant. Have you thought about opening an office here? They could sure use another one. My dad has a farm outside of town and is struggling with his books. He's already had trouble with the IRS and is panicking."

"I, uh, was planning to move to Austin in a few weeks. I'm not sure Riverbend is the place for me."

"Why not? You said yourself that everyone has been real friendly to you." Rita's consultant returned and tsked at her.

"You've been talking. Your mask is cracked."

"Sorry."

"No more talking until I take it off."

Caitlyn was secretly relieved that Rita had been warned to stop talking. She was making Caitlyn uncomfortable, probably because she was beginning to feel sorry for some of the people who were having trouble. If not for her, Brian would have been in the same boat. Still, she was sure living close to her brother would be a disaster waiting to happen. She didn't want a strained relationship between them. They were all each other had.

She was certain that Rita would have forgotten what she had been talking about by the time they were finished with the facial part of the spa treatment, so she was surprised when she took up where she had left off once the mask was rinsed off.

"I know that some of the business owners around here have to take their stuff to other towns. Just think, you could live here, maybe meet someone and settle down."

"I'm not looking to settle down with anyone right now," she said.

"Well, you can still open your office here."

After that, they talked about the upcoming ceremonies and Tish confessed that she was more nervous about the private one with both of her men than she was about the official one.

"I mean, it's just for show, really. Brian and Andy both insisted that I marry Brian so that I'd have his last name for the children. I don't see why it should matter."

"You will have a little more security this way in case something happens to Brian." Rita tried to explain the reason behind it.

"Still, I feel like I'm slighting Andy. He assures me that he's fine with it and thinks it's the best idea." Tish frowned.

"What worries you about the private ceremony?" Caitlyn changed the subject, hoping to get her mind off of the legal ceremony.

"I want it to be perfect and I'm scared the cake isn't going to be right or something will happen to mess it up, like it will rain." They were having the ceremony outside behind Brian and Andy's house.

"It's not supposed to rain for several days," Rita supplied.

"And the cake is going to be perfect." Caitlyn decided Tish was working herself up over nothing. "You're going to look beautiful in your dress and the men will fall in love with you all over again."

"That's so romantic of you to say," Tish said. "Thanks."

"That's because you've made my brother very happy. For that I'll always be grateful. He deserves to be happy."

Once they were finished, it was just after five. She hesitated at going back to Lamar and Brody's house right away in case they weren't home yet. They had told her where a key was kept, but she didn't feel comfortable being alone in their house. She would be uncomfortable until they got there.

She took her time perusing the stores next to the spa before climbing into her SUV and driving toward their house. She decided when she was only a half mile away that she would drive by first to see if they were home. They had taken separate trucks that morning. If at least one of them proved to be there, she would turn around and go back.

To her relief, both trucks were there. She turned around and pulled into the drive. Still, she hesitated getting out of the car. She knew she was on the verge of falling for them. It scared her because she really felt like moving to Austin was the best option for her.

The door to the house opened and Lamar walked out with a puzzled expression on his face. He walked over to the SUV and cocked his head.

Caitlyn grabbed her purse and opened the door to get out.

"Hey, is something wrong?"

"No, I was just thinking."

"About whether you wanted to come inside or not?"

"No, just thinking about life in general. Nothing in particular." She walked ahead of him toward the door so that he couldn't see her face. She knew she didn't lie well.

When she got to the door, Brody had already opened it. His face didn't show anything of what he was thinking. If he had found it strange that she'd been sitting in her car in the drive, she couldn't tell it. Guilt tightened her stomach.

"Did you have a good time at the spa?" he asked.

"It was definitely an experience. I enjoyed the manicure and pedicure, but I think I could have done without the two different kinds of mud they smeared on me."

"Mud?" Lamar shook his head. "I thought they were purifying your skin, not putting dirt on it."

She couldn't help but laugh. He had a look of distaste on his face. She had felt almost the same way while they were applying it.

"Are you hungry? Lamar thought we would grill steaks out." Brody watched her almost as if he expected her to turn around and leave.

"Steaks sound good." She turned to Lamar. "Need help with anything?"

"Nope, I've got it covered. How do you like your steak cooked?"

"Medium is fine, thanks."

"Come on, Caity. You can pick out movies to watch tonight." Brody steered her toward the living room with a hand to her back.

"You already know that we've got quite a few DVDs to choose from. Some of them we've never even seen. I think Lamar stopped by the store and bought a few more."

"I'd rather watch something that you've never watched, so tell me if you've already have."

She found the new ones without a problem because they still had the plastic on them. Two of them were comedies and the other two were action thrillers. She pulled them off of the shelf and handed them to Brody. He glanced at them and grunted. She assumed that meant that he was okay with them. With him, it was hard to tell what he thought when he was in one of his moods, as she thought of them.

"Steaks should be ready soon. He has baked potatoes to go with them."

"Great. I'm sort of hungry. They served wine and cheese to us at the spa, but I'm still hungry."

"Good. He'll feel slighted if you don't eat."

Caitlyn felt like they were making small talk. His speech was a bit stilted. It worried her. Something was going on with him.

"Brody, is my staying here tonight really okay with you? You don't seem very comfortable."

He dropped his head back on his shoulders and looked up. Then his lips thinned and he looked back at her.

"It's not that. We've got some things going on at work that have me on edge. It's absolutely fine that you're here. I want you here. Lamar wants you here." He huffed out a breath.

"Is there something I can help with? Is it about your bookkeeping or taxes?"

He pulled her into his arms and hugged her close.

"Thanks, but it doesn't have anything to do with the books or taxes. It's customer related. I'm sorry I brought it home with me. I'm not used to there being anyone here other than Lamar, and we usually talk about work whenever we want to."

"You shouldn't have to change your routine for me, Brody. I don't want to cause trouble by being here."

"You're not causing any trouble." He pushed her away so that he could look down at her. "You belong here with us. I wish you would realize that."

"Brody, don't push me. I already worry that seeing each other is going to be a problem in the long run."

He let go of her and ran one hand through his hair. He looked like he was going to say something, but Lamar walked in and announced that dinner was ready. Brody let it go but the look on his face said that he wouldn't forget about it. He would bring it back up later.

They ate at the kitchen table since there was more room than there was on the bar. Lamar had grilled her steak perfectly. She managed to eat it all and most of her potato, which obviously pleased him.

"We've got ice cream and a lemon pie for dessert," he said when they had finished.

"I can't eat anything else right now. Maybe later." She stood up and began gathering the dishes.

"I've got them. You go and relax in the living room. We'll be right there." Lamar gave her a little push toward the other room.

Caitlyn left them dealing with the dishes and sat on the couch to wait on them. She leaned her head back and closed her eyes. Immediately, images of the three of them in bed appeared in her head.

She realized that she had slowly gotten aroused just being around them. If they affected her so easily, they would soon have her begging for sex. She couldn't let that happen. As soon as the wedding was over, she needed to pull away from them before someone got hurt. She figured she would be the one hurt in the long run.

A good fifteen minutes passed before they sat down on the couch on either side of her. She started, opening her eyes wide to find them watching her. Brody still wore a strained look on his face but now, Lamar did, too. It was unusual for him to look so serious. What had they talked about in the kitchen while they were cleaning up the dishes? Did she really want to know? Yeah. She figured it had to do with her and whatever it was, they had argued about it. That was something she didn't want to happen. It was why she didn't think a ménage relationship would work. Now she had all the proof she needed.

Chapter Thirteen

Brody had been brooding over the problem with their bids on projects. For some reason, most of them came back as refused. They'd never had a problem like that before. Ever since they had found out he and Lamar had been trying to get to the bottom of the problem. So far all they had found out was that someone was undermining their credibility and the quality of their work. It was frustrating and beginning to hurt their business and the bottom line.

He looked over at Caitlyn as she watched the movie. He needed to put it out of his mind while they had her there with them. She was obviously picking up on his stress. She naturally would think it had to do with her. Having her there with them was soothing in a way. He just had to concentrate on the time they had with her. He had no doubt she was going to leave. Lamar still had hope, but he was more realistic. No matter how hard they tried to convince her she belonged with them, her past was in the way. She was probably right. It was too soon for her to have put it behind her.

Right now, they had her sitting between them on the couch. He had his hand on her thigh because he had to touch her. Lamar seemed to be the same way since he had his arm across her shoulders. Brody was drawn to her like a moth to a flame. She seemed to lift some of the darkness he often felt was inside of him.

Now that they'd had her with them, he wondered how he would be able to handle losing her presence in their lives. Sure, they could see her occasionally in Austin when they drove over there, but it wouldn't be the same, and it wouldn't last long.

The movie was coming to an end. He waited until the last possible minute to move his hand to grab the remote to the DVD player.

"That was a really good movie." She stretched, dislodging Lamar's arm from her shoulders in the process.

Brody turned off the DVD player and changed the channel on the TV to one that had something besides paid advertising on it. He looked back at her and couldn't help but smile because she was smiling.

"Yeah, it was a good movie. Both of them were."

"It's close to midnight. I'm ready for bed." Lamar stood up before reaching down and grabbing Caitlyn's hand.

"Sounds good to me." Brody took her other hand, and they pulled her to her feet.

"Slow down, you two. Your legs are longer than mine."

They both slowed down, making sure not to pull her along anymore. Brody hadn't thought about anything other than getting her in bed. No doubt Lamar had been thinking the same thing.

Once they were upstairs in the bedroom, he turned and reached for her. She smiled and took a step back. He liked the playful side of her. He was usually all business, but it was nice to loosen up some.

He stalked her as she backed away from him until he had her pinned to the wall. Her eyes widened when he stepped into her personal space and cupped her cheek in his hand. There was nothing that he wanted more than to bury himself so far inside of her that she couldn't imagine him not being there.

"I want you, Caity. I want you so badly I can't think right now."

"Yes." Her voice came out breathy. His cock, already hard, tightened more behind the zipper of his jeans.

He was vaguely aware of Lamar pulling the covers to the end of the bed and throwing the pillows to the floor. Brody wanted both of them to take her at the same time tonight. Something told him that the timing was important. He felt like she was on the cusp with her emotions concerning them.

"We want you." He clarified his statement. "Both of us want to make love to you at the same time. Will you let us?"

He watched her eyes widen then darken with arousal. He had his answer. She wanted the same thing.

"I've never done that before."

"Have two men at the same time?" he asked.

"That or had anal sex. I don't know if I can."

Lamar spoke up from where he was waiting at the side of the bed. "We'll go slowly. We would never hurt you, Caity. If you say stop, we'll stop."

"Give us a chance to show you pleasure like you've never felt before." Brody held his breath as she thought about it.

When she said *yes*, he let it out in a whoosh. He made short work of ridding her of her clothes. Lamar was busy undressing himself. Only Brody still had his clothes on when he picked her up and carried her to the bed. He gently laid her down then backed away to pull off his clothes. His brother took that opportunity to zero in on her breasts. He watched him lick and suck at her nipples as he finished undressing. The sight had his already rock-hard cock jumping with his heartbeat.

He wanted to make her come first, but knew that would leave her swollen, making it more difficult for them to work their way inside of her. Instead, they would play with her until she was on the verge so that she would need to come so badly that the slight pain she would feel wouldn't matter.

"Lamar, get a condom on."

Caitlyn whimpered when his brother let go of her nipple with a soft *pop*. She reached for him as he pulled away to reach a condom in the bedside table drawer. He pulled out two and fished out the lube while he was in there. Tossing one of the condoms and the lube to Brody, Lamar tore open the condom and quickly rolled it on his thick dick. He ran his hand up and down it a couple of times as he watched Caitlyn's face.

"Caity, climb on Lamar and ride him. I want to watch your hot pussy suck him inside of you." Brody smoothed down his condom over his cock and grasped the base and squeezed as Caitlyn crawled over Lamar's prone body.

He drew in a deep breath as she slowly lowered her body over Lamar's dick. Her pussy lips separated as she inched down the thick cock, stretching her slit wide to accommodate Lamar's extreme width. The sight of her cunt spreading wide for Lamar had him swallowing and grasping his cock tighter as he pumped up and down it. He stopped before he lost it.

"Your pussy is so pretty and pink wrapped around Lamar's dick."

"He fills me up inside. It almost hurts, he's so big."

"Just wait until I get inside of you, too. You're going to be so full of cock you won't know what to do."

Brody took the lube and pressed lightly on her back to get her to lie flat on top of Lamar. She obeyed without asking. He reveled in her acceptance of his dominance.

"You're going to feel something cold back here, baby. Just relax and let me work you open. I'm going to play with this little hole back here."

She wiggled her ass, much to Lamar's frustration by the sound of it. His brother groaned and reached up to hold her still.

"Don't move, Caity. I don't want to come yet."

Brody suppressed a chuckle. He knew his brother wouldn't appreciate it. Instead, he dribbled a small amount of lube on the little pucker of her ass. She stiffened for just a second, and then relaxed again. He spread the jelly around her back hole before applying a little pressure until just the tip of one finger breached it. He moved it in and out the tiniest bits before withdrawing it and applying more lube.

This time he pressed against the dark rosette until she was taking him to the first knuckle. She moaned when he pressed a little deeper to his second knuckle. He waited for her to adjust to him. Then he pumped his finger in and out until she was easily accepting him to the webbing of his hand.

"How are you doing, Caity?" He wanted to be sure she was all right.

"I'm fine. It's not really hurting. It just feels weird."

"Good. I'm going to add another finger."

She shivered all over. Lamar groaned.

Brody added more lube before adding a second finger to the first. She resisted him at first, but when he massaged her lower back and talked to her, she slowly relaxed and let him in.

"Good girl. Just relax. Push out when I push in."

"Oh, God, it stings. I need to move, Brody."

"Don't move, baby. You'll set Lamar off. Just concentrate on relaxing and letting me in."

He felt her relax her ass as he carefully slid both fingers all the way in. Then he carefully moved them in and out of her until she was trying to push back to meet him. He figured she was as ready as she was going to get now. He removed his fingers earning him a moan.

After applying a liberal amount of the jelly to his sheathed cock, Brody positioned himself at her back hole and slowly pushed. She whimpered but he could tell she was pushing back against him. She didn't ask him to stop. Pressing a little harder, he finally breached her tight ring with the head of his dick.

"Oh, God! You're so big."

"Are you okay, baby?" Lamar asked in a strained voice.

"Yes. How much more?"

"I'm just barely inside of you, Caity. Do I need to stop?"

"No. I'm okay. Just hurry."

Brody pulled back a little then surged forward into her tight hole. After a few more pushes, he was all the way inside of her and stopped moving to give her time to adjust to his being inside of her at the same time Lamar was. He knew she would feel full of cock.

"Please, Brody. You've got to move. I can't stand it. Move!"

Brody smiled. He pulled out and pushed forward as Lamar pulled out and returned. They set a rhythm so that one of them filled her at all times. She tried to rock with them, but Brody stopped her.

"Easy, baby. Let us do the work. Just feel. Feel us loving you. God, you're squeezing my dick so hard it almost hurts."

"It burns. I need more, Brody, Lamar. Faster." Her breathy voice was music to his ears.

They sped up until each of them tunneled in and out of her, rushing toward their climax. He wanted her to come first. He needed to hear her reach hers before they did. She was all that mattered in that instant. Everything rested on her pleasure. Brody broke out in a sweat as he staved off his orgasm, praying that Lamar would be able to hold on just a little longer. She had to come first.

* * * *

Caitlyn mewed as the pressure built inside of her. The pleasure-pain of Brody fucking her in the ass only added to the sweet pressure that was growing deep inside her cunt, spreading out to the rest of her body with each stroke of their cocks inside of her.

Lamar's dick rasped over her sweet spot with each plunge, sending tentacles of warmth throughout her bloodstream. Her cunt was alive with sensation.

Brody's cock had awakened nerve endings inside her ass that she never knew existed before that moment. Her ass was on fire as every stroke of his dick built her pleasure until she thought she would explode with it. She tried to push back against him to urge him faster, harder, but he wouldn't change his rhythm. Frustrated, Caitlyn whimpered as she curled her hands tighter over Lamar's shoulders. She squeezed down on both men in an effort to speed up their orgasms, anything to end the need burning inside her bloodstream.

"Fuck, baby. Don't do that. I want you to come before I do." Lamar grunted when she did it again.

"You're playing with fire, Caity." Brody pulled her ass cheeks farther apart as he stroked his cock in and out of her back hole.

Now the pleasure was growing too fast. She didn't think she could handle it. It would kill her if she came like this. It was too much, too soon.

"I can't do it. Please, it's too much."

"It's not. Let it happen. Fly for us, baby." Brody slammed into her over and over.

Lamar reached up and pulled on her nipples, sending sparks flying through her body. She ignited into pleasure so intense that it was almost painful. Explosions rippled through her cunt and fire raced through her veins sending wave after wave of sensation pounding into her as hard as the men were thrusting inside of her.

Even in the throes of her orgasm, she knew when they lost their rhythm and began to fill their condoms with scalding hot cum. Together they rode the waves of pleasure until they all collapsed. In that instant, Caitlyn knew she had lost the fight and had fallen in love with them. They had filled her body with their cocks, but they had also filled her heart with their loving.

She gasped for breath even as tears slid from her eyes to wet Lamar's chest. A sweet pain burned her soul with the knowledge that they had no real future together. She would be leaving in the next two and a half or three weeks. They might come see her for awhile, but eventually they would tire of the trips and stop altogether.

All of this drifted through her mind as she lay there listening to the rapid beat of Lamar's heart. Brody slowly pulled from her body and her sweat-soaked skin cooled in the night air. When he returned, it was to clean her up with a damp cloth. Then they lifted her off of Lamar and settled her under the covers between them. Their tender care was almost more than she could handle. Thank goodness they hadn't realized she was crying. She let the tears flow until sleep finally claimed her.

Chapter Fourteen

Caitlyn stood outside at her brother's house while he, Andy, and Tish said their vows to each other. It was a beautiful ceremony made even more so by the fact that the two men were obviously in love with Tish. She was equally in love with them by the soft glow on her face and the smile in her eyes.

They had already had the legal wedding between Tish and Brian. Andy had been Brian's best man. It all seemed so surreal to Caitlyn. Before Brian had announced he was living in a ménage relationship, she'd never heard of such a thing. Sure, she knew about ménages, but she had always assumed they were just a sex thing. Now she knew better.

Even as the three exchanged their promises, she thought about Brody and Lamar who were standing just behind her among the select guests. She loved them. Nothing had prepared her for the real deal. Her supposed marriage to Harold had been a farce in more ways than one. She'd believed herself in love with him but soon realized that it wasn't love. Now she knew what love felt like. Right then, it hurt.

The ceremony came to an end with Brian and Andy exchanging kisses with Tish. Caitlyn pasted a smile on her face because she didn't want Brian to worry about her. They would leave on their honeymoon after the reception and she would be able to relax her guard. She would return to their home to house-sit and handle their business until they returned. Then she would move to Austin like she had planned and get on with her life. People lived with a broken heart all the time. So could she.

"What's wrong, Caity?" Lamar whispered in her ear.

"Nothing."

"Yes, there is. You may have a smile on your face, but your eyes are sad."

"Brian, Andy, and Tish are happy together. Don't worry about them." Brody leaned in on the other side of her.

"I know they are. It's obvious they're in love by the look on their faces."

"Then what's making you sad?" Lamar asked.

She struggled to think of something to say that would placate them. Nothing came to mind.

"I guess too much has happened lately. My baby brother is married. He's all grown up."

"Feeling sentimental?" Brody watched her closely.

"I guess so."

"I'm not buying it. Something else is wrong."

Caitlyn looked to Lamar for help, but he looked at her with an odd expression on his face. He looked disappointed for some reason. He sighed and shook his head.

"She's already thinking about leaving," he said.

"You're still here for three weeks. Don't think for one minute that we're going to let you push us away." Brody's anger was a palpable thing.

The heat of it burned along her skin, leaving a trail of sadness in its wake. She felt tears stinging the back of her eyes and worked to keep them from falling. She wouldn't ruin her brother's reception by crying.

"Brody, don't do this here. I can't deal with it right now."

"We will talk, Caitlyn. As soon as they leave on their honeymoon we're going back to the house and deal with it there."

She couldn't say anything. She was afraid she would burst out crying if she did. She nodded and hurried over to Tish to hug her and wish her well. She could pass her tears off as tears of happiness for them.

Relieved that Brody and Lamar didn't follow her, she pulled her sister-in-law into a brief hug.

"The ceremony was beautiful, Tish. I'm so happy for you and the guys."

"Thanks. Don't cry, silly." She brushed away Caitlyn's tears and laughed. "If Brian sees you crying he's going to think something is wrong."

"I always cry at weddings, and this one is my baby brother's."

"Thank you for taking care of everything for us." Tish squeezed her hands.

"I don't mind at all. You know that. It will be fun to wrap things up and mail them. It will be almost like Christmas."

"Still, it takes a lot of pressure off of Brian. He and Andy need this vacation after all the hard work they've put into everything."

"Well, don't forget it's your honeymoon, too."

"Don't worry, we won't let her forget." Brian and Andy walked up. They each wrapped her in a hug.

Brian looked at her and frowned. "Are you crying?"

"I can't help it. The ceremony was so nice."

He grinned and draped his arm over her shoulders. "You could have one, too, sis."

She stiffened before she could stop herself. He looked at her with speculation. Then he changed the subject.

The afternoon grew late as everyone helped Tish, Brian, and Andy celebrate their marriage. Caitlyn helped with the refreshments and watched as her brother and his new family danced and circulated among their friends.

After a while Brian pulled them over to where she was standing.

"Looks like we can make our getaway, guys. I'm ready to get out of this monkey suit and get on the road."

Andy took Tish's hand and the three of them slipped inside the house, leaving the guests milling about in the yard. They would all gather at the drive in an hour and throw birdseed at them as they made a mad dash to get in the truck and leave. They had already packed their belongings in it.

She grabbed another glass of champagne and sipped it as she waited for the three newlyweds to emerge from the house. Time seemed to stand still. She began to worry that they would never come out when the front door finally opened and they ran for the truck. Despite catching many of the guests off guard, it didn't save them from handfuls of birdseed raining down on them. She had little doubt they would find it in their hair, clothes, and the car when they arrived at their destination.

As their car drove away, she began to help Rita clean up and thank the guests for coming. She was surprised to see Brody and Lamar helping to straighten up the backyard, carrying the folding tables to their truck to return to the rental store. Once everything was loaded that had been rented, Brody and another man she didn't know took it back.

Lamar stayed close to her while she finished cleaning up. Then he steered her inside the house once everyone had left and they were alone.

"Brody will be back soon. Then we'll head home."

She didn't bother arguing with him. They needed to have the talk before things went any further. Then she would insist they bring her back to Brian's place. More than likely they would be glad to do it. She had little doubt that Brody's temperament would accept her decision to leave as soon as her brother and the others returned from their honeymoon. Tish had caught on fast to the bookkeeping and record-keeping programs she had set up for them. She wouldn't need any further education.

She took a seat in the living room and leaned her head back against the back of the couch. She was exhausted from all the preparations and the added emotional stress she was under. If she could have lain down, Caitlyn had little doubt that she would have fallen asleep.

"You look tired."

"It's been a very eventful day. Thank goodness for Rita. I couldn't have done everything without her."

"She's a nice woman. I've known her for years. She runs a little boutique in town. I think it sells woman's underwear."

"I think I've been in it. I found a couple of things there."

"Maybe you could model them for me later." Lamar waggled his eyebrows at her.

She couldn't help but laugh at his antics.

"That's better. I was afraid your face was going to freeze with that silly frown on your mouth." He pulled her down on the couch and hugged her.

"What are you still doing here? Why didn't you leave with Brody and the other guy? I'm sure they could have used your help in unloading everything."

"I won the coin toss and got Caity duty." He grinned at her before pulling her over so that her head rested on his shoulder.

Nearly twenty minutes later, Brody walked into the house. He stared at them for a few seconds then sighed.

"Let's go. Lock up, Lamar. I'll carry her out to the truck." Brody reached down to pick her up.

"I can walk. I have a headache and was resting my head." She really did have a headache.

"I'll carry you. Have you taken anything for your head yet?" He swung her up in his arms without a problem.

"No. I didn't feel like moving."

She clutched his shoulders, knowing he could carry her without a problem. It felt good to be in his arms, a sort of sweet torture. Resting her head on Lamar's shoulder had felt much the same way.

Brody eased her inside the truck and fastened her in. A minute later, Lamar climbed up beside her. The slamming of the doors caused her to wince. Her headache was getting worse all the time. Maybe she'd had too much champagne. She only remembered having a glass and a half. More than likely it was the strain of dealing with the weddings and her situation.

When they pulled up outside their house, the two men climbed out of the truck. Lamar unfastened her seat belt and scooped her up in his arms, carrying her in the house when Brody unlocked it. They went straight upstairs, Brody taking her from Lamar's arms to climb the stairs. Then Lamar was handing her a glass of water and two pain tablets. She swallowed them without a fuss.

She hardly noticed when they stripped her and put her to bed. The pounding in her head slowly eased up enough that she was able to think again. Thinking wasn't a good idea. The fact that she was in love with two men kept circling in her head. Not only was she sure it would never work, but she was positive that she needed to move to Austin to start over.

She didn't think she could start over in Riverbend with Brian living there as well. They argued constantly when they were around each other too much. Then there was Brody and Lamar. Despite loving them like she did, she wasn't ready to step into a serious relationship with anyone. Not even the two men she loved. It was too soon. The hurt was too fresh.

Finally, she drifted off to sleep with thoughts of the two men fueling her dreams.

* * * *

She woke up the next morning to an empty bed. She could tell they had slept with her by the indentions on the pillows. Though the headache was gone, she felt slightly off kilter. She couldn't tell if it was because she wasn't quite awake yet or if it was a residual of the headache still hanging around.

She looked around for a clock but couldn't find one. She wasn't wearing a watch, and her cell phone was in her purse, which wasn't in the room. After sitting on the edge of the bed for a few seconds, she decided she was steady enough to stand up. The world didn't tilt, so she walked to the bathroom. When she emerged from the bathroom wrapped in a towel, it was to find Lamar sitting on the edge of the bed waiting on her.

"Good morning. How is your head?"

"It's better, thank you. I'm still a little groggy. I thought a shower would help, but I guess the headache left me feeling this way."

"Are you hungry?"

"Not really. I'm not sure I could eat anything right now. A cup of coffee would be wonderful, though."

"I'll get some for you while you dress." He stood up and walked out of the room without touching her.

She pulled on sweatpants and a T-shirt from her bag. She didn't really feel like dressing at all. Maybe all that was wrong with her was that she didn't want to have that talk Brody had insisted they were going to have. Did that make her a coward? Probably.

Lamar walked back in carrying a cup. He handed it to her and waited there while she sipped it. The hot liquid warmed her from the inside out but didn't touch the cold that seemed to encase her soul now.

"Ready to go downstairs?"

She started, having forgotten that Lamar was waiting on her. Caitlyn nodded and followed behind as he led the way down the stairs. When he continued into the kitchen, she wondered if Brody was in there. But when she walked in the room it was to find that he wasn't. She wondered where he was. It was Sunday. Surely he hadn't gone into work.

Finally she got up the nerve to ask Lamar where he was.

"He's in the office. I think he's trying to figure out your system so he can follow it."

"I'll teach you both as soon as I finish setting it up."

"Are you going to have time? I mean, you're planning on leaving when Brian, Andy, and Tish get back, aren't you?"

"I'll be sure you have what you need before I leave." She swallowed hard around the lump in her throat.

Lamar's carefully neutral expression and comments hurt. But what did she expect? She was leaving.

She finished her coffee and rinsed the cup in the sink before setting it on the counter. Then she turned to Lamar and waited to see what was next.

"Do you feel like working on the books some more?"

"Yes. I want to get them in order for you."

Lamar didn't say anything. Instead he walked out of the kitchen toward the office. She followed him determined to ignore his attitude. It was more like Brody's than his.

Caitlyn walked into the office to find Brody standing in front of the window looking out at the backyard. She had no idea what he was looking at or if it was even anything out there. The stiff set of his shoulders told her all she needed to know. They were both angry.

She walked over to the desk and sat down to finish entering figures into the program she'd set up on their computer. No one said anything for a long time. Then Brody turned from the window and watched her as she worked. It was unnerving. She started to ask him to stop it when he started talking.

"We need to talk, Caitlyn. As soon as you finish what you're doing, come into the living room." Then he turned and left the room with Lamar right behind him.

Anger finally broke through the hurt, giving her the strength to follow them. She saved her work and walked into the living room. They looked up, their surprise at seeing her written on their face. She planted her hands on her hips and glared at the two men.

"What have I done to deserve the way you're treating me? I never promised you anything. In fact, I told you from the beginning that I was moving to Austin and a relationship between us would only lead to disaster. I was right. That's where we are right now, in the middle of a disaster."

She stopped, realizing that she was panting from the adrenaline running through her veins. No doubt when it gave out, she'd collapse. She wanted to be gone by that time. She refused to break down in front of them. She would walk to Brian's house if she had to.

"I told you it was too soon. It's been less than six months. We've only known each other for a week. Yet you expect me to open a business here and date the two of you as if it's the most normal thing in the world. I've already told you that I can't be what you need."

"You're wrong, Caitlyn. You can be what we need. But you're right. We don't have the right to treat you like we have. You never promised us anything. We refused to believe you wouldn't change your mind, that we couldn't change your mind." Brody stood up and walked over to her.

He sighed and pulled her into his arms. She stiffened, not sure what was going on.

"I'm sorry. Maybe we should talk now rather than later."

Caitlyn pulled back as far as he would let her go. "I'm not sure we have anything to talk about. I'm going back to Brian's house."

"Wait and hear us out. Then if you still want to go, I'll drive you there."

She looked into his eyes but only saw worry and perhaps sadness. Even though he'd pissed her off, she was sorry that she'd put it there.

He drew her over to the couch and gently pushed her down to take a seat. Lamar got up and walked across the room to stand in front of the TV. He looked tired. It seemed she would have to listen to whatever they had to say whether she wanted to or not. Fine. Then she could go to Brian's.

"Caity, we don't want you to go, but I realize you probably will anyway. You're right. What you went through takes time to heal and you haven't had long enough to get past it yet. Lamar and I care about you more than I can explain to you." He took a deep breath then let it out slowly.

"When you get ready to move, I hope you will let us help you. We want to keep seeing you in Austin. Don't shut us out."

Caitlyn wasn't sure what to say. She hadn't expected him to give in so easily. The fact that he seemed to want to keep seeing her spoke volumes as to how much he cared. She looked over at Lamar. He still looked sad, but now she saw hope. How could she say no when all she wanted to do was say yes and hold on to them for as long as she could?

"No pressure?"

"No pressure. But we will keep showing you just how good we are together and how much we want you."

"I care about the two of you, too. Probably more than I'm comfortable with. I'll let you help me move when I get ready to. First I have to find a job. Then I'll look for a place to live."

"And you'll go out with us when we come to Austin?" Brody stuck his hands in his pocket.

"I'll go out with you." God, she hoped she wasn't making a mistake.

"We want you to stay with us while you're still here."

"I'm supposed to be house-sitting for Brian."

"We'll help you keep an eye on it, but he really doesn't need anyone to watch it here in Riverbend. No one will bother it."

Caitlyn bit her lower lip and thought about it. They were probably right about not needing a house sitter. Still, staying there with them seemed like a bad idea. They would get used to having her around and when she left, it would be a shock.

"Are you sure you want me to? It will make my leaving in three weeks that much harder for all of us."

"Stay, Caity. We want you near us as much as possible." This time Lamar spoke up.

"Okay, I'll stay. I'm probably going to regret it, but I can't say no."

Lamar's face changed from the tense expression she wasn't used to, to one of relief and pleasure. She liked that one on him much better. Looking toward Brody, Caitlyn was able to see a change in him as well. He kept his emotions hidden for the most part, but his eyes held relief as well.

"Let's go get the rest of your things from their house." Lamar didn't seem to want to take any chances that she would change her mind.

"After lunch will be soon enough, Lamar." Brody either trusted her or was just that practical.

She stood up and Lamar immediately crossed to her, wrapping his arms around her.

"You promise you'll stay with us until the three weeks are up?"

"I promise. But I am going to move, Lamar. You need to remember that."

"And we're going to try to change your mind so remember that." He looked across at Brody.

Brody nodded but didn't say anything. Sometimes his silences were more telling than words. His eyes spoke volumes, telling her that he didn't plan on giving up either. She shivered. The next three weeks were going to be some of the most exciting and the most stressful times of her life. She just hoped she was up to the challenge.

Lamar fixed sandwiches for lunch and Caitlyn worked on their books until then. As soon as they finished lunch, he pushed her outside and into the truck. Brody smiled and shook his head at her silent appeal for help. She was still chewing her last bite of food.

They loaded her things up in their truck and Lamar drove her SUV back to their house for her. She had argued that she could drive it herself but had been outnumbered, so Lamar drove. They unpacked for her, putting everything away as if she were moving in for good. Nothing she had said seemed to thwart them. She finally returned to the office to work and left them to it. She would have preferred living out of her suitcases. It would have made packing up to leave much easier, in more ways than one.

"I wondered where you'd gotten off to." Brody walked into the room carrying a glass of what looked like iced tea.

"Is that for me?"

"Depends."

"On what?"

"If you make it worth my while."

She cocked an eyebrow at him. "Just what did you have in mind?"

"Just a kiss." He waggled his brows back at her.

"I think I can manage that. Can I taste the tea first to see if it's worth one?"

"No, you're just going to have to take my word for it. It's good." He walked around the desk and set the glass on a coaster then leaned down toward her.

Caitlyn knew it wouldn't be just a kiss. Brody didn't do anything in half measures. Add to that the fact that they were trying to convince her that she belonged with them, and the kiss had the potential to be spectacular. And she was right. It was one hell of a kiss.

He sipped at her lips before drawing in the bottom one to suck on. He nipped it then licked it and moved deeper into her mouth. She moaned at the taste of him. The flavor of warm coffee and tangy toothpaste filled her senses. He licked along the roof of her mouth before sliding his tongue along hers.

When he slowly pulled away, they were both panting and she was squirming in her seat, her panties wet with her excitement. She couldn't stop the small spasms in her pussy that threatened to turn her into a wanton woman, begging him for sex, right then and right there. Somehow, she figured he would welcome the chance to spill all her careful paperwork to the floor to clear the desk for their use.

"I like whatever you're thinking about, Caity. Your face just turned all shades of pink and red and your eyes got dark. Are you picturing us on the desk with my cock buried so deep in your cunt that you can't move?"

Brody chuckled at her deepening embarrassment. No doubt her fair complexion showed every shade of red by now. She wanted to punch him for catching her off guard. Instead, she reached around him and grabbed the glass of iced tea. She accidentally brushed it against his side where his T-shirt rode up on his back. He yelped and jerked away. Caitlyn only just managed to save the tea from being dropped on the floor.

While she sipped her tea, Brody dried the spot off with a paper towel from the roll they kept there in the office. She had no idea what they used it for, but decided not to ask. Instead she set the glass back on the coaster and settled back in the chair to get back to work. Her wet panties and flashbacks to the night before made it all but impossible to concentrate. Evidently Brody noticed.

"You've been staring at that same screen without doing anything for five minutes. Are you looking for something in particular?" He leaned over her shoulder, his breath warm against her ear.

"I was thinking. Move back. I don't like anyone looking over my shoulder."

He chuckled. "You're *thinking* about us. Maybe if you took a little break you could come back refreshed later."

"If I take a little break, we'll end up in bed and I might not make it back downstairs at all."

"If I promise we won't end up in bed, will you take a break?"

Caitlyn sighed and dropped her head on the computer keyboard. The computer dinged at her, and she sat back up.

"Okay, a short break." She stood up and let him lead her out the door and back toward the living room. Lamar was standing in front of the shelves looking at the DVDs. He turned around when he heard them walk in.

"You found her."

"She was pretending to work in the office."

"Hey! I was working just fine until you interrupted me."

Lamar chuckled. "I was looking for a movie. Any preferences?"

"Something short. I'm only taking a short break from working on your books. I have a long way to getting them in decent shape."

"A short one it is." He selected one from the shelves and popped it into the DVD player. Then he sat down on the couch and patted the cushion next to him. "Have a seat."

Brody followed her and sat on the other side of her. They each took one of her hands and held it as the previews started on the TV. Brody ran his thumb around the palm of her hand in slow circles. Lamar laced his fingers in with hers. Warmth from each of their hands began to seep into her skin. She was so caught up in their hands that she missed the opening of the first scene in the movie.

Brody's thumb moved to her wrist, where it stroked along her pulse. Lamar's warm, hard thigh rested alongside hers, sending another shot of heat to her aching pussy. Damn, she was turned on and they hadn't really done anything. Well, that wasn't exactly true. Brody had started it all with the kiss. Now she was stuck like a cat in heat with a room full of neutered males because she'd told Brody that she didn't want to end up in bed.

Brody leaned over and whispered in her ear. "Having trouble concentrating on the movie, Caitydid?"

"Screw you, Brody." She'd be damned if she would give him the satisfaction of suggesting sex.

"You're squirming too much for me to enjoy the movie."

Lamar leaned over and shushed them. "I can't hear the movie with you two talking."

Caitlyn frowned at him before she wiggled to find a more comfortable position. Nothing was comfortable with a wet pussy and an aching cunt.

Lamar gave her innocent eyes, but she saw the quick exchange of looks between him and Brody. They were playing her like a well-tuned piano.

"Maybe I can help you get comfortable." Lamar reached over with one hand and unfastened her jeans before she knew what he was up to.

"Brody! I said no sex."

"No, you didn't. You said you weren't going to end up in bed and I agreed. We're not in bed."

"It's the same thing," she hissed out.

"No, it's not. This is couch sex and much more difficult to achieve safely."

Lamar stood up and unfastened his jeans, shoving them down his thighs to his ankles. His dick sprang up as if waiting for the chance to get out. His cockhead was a ruddy red, and the vein running along the top stood out, a blue contrast to the almost angry-looking red of the skin.

"Suck my cock, Caity."

She licked her lips, unable to take her eyes off of the thick meat only a few feet away from her watering mouth. She started to lean over, but Brody grabbed her by the hair and stopped her.

"Wait a minute. I have an idea where we'll all be satisfied. Caity, stand up and lean over the arm of the couch. Lamar, scoot to the end so that she can reach you." Brody directed them to where he wanted them.

She quickly got up and walked around the end of the couch where she bent over the arm, her jean-clad ass in the air. While Lamar moved over to the end of the couch, Brody pulled her jeans down and had her step out of them after she toed off her shoes.

Lamar grabbed the back of her head and pulled her down within licking distance of his dick. She reached out with her tongue and ran it across the top and across the slit where a drop of cum had beaded up. She hummed her approval and began to lick all around the cockhead. Caitlyn looked up to watch his face as she sucked just the head of him into her mouth. His eyes closed, and he threw back his head against the back of the couch.

She felt Brody's sheathed cock probing her entrance from behind and widened her stance to give him more room. Moisture leaked from her pussy to run down her thigh as he rubbed his dick up and down her slit. She tried to follow him with her body, but he popped her ass with a hand.

"Be still, Caity. I'm handling this pretty pussy just fine. I don't need your help back here."

She rolled her eyes but stopped trying to force him inside of her. Instead, she concentrated on driving Lamar crazy. She wanted to send him over hard enough that he wouldn't be able to stand up for a while. Using just the tip of her tongue, she ran it up the length of his dick and back down on the other side. Then she sucked him down hard and fast, taking him to the back of her throat where she swallowed around him.

"Fuck! That's it, baby. Suck it all."

She backed off him, letting her teeth rasp over the delicate tissue of his cock. Since she had to use her hands to hold herself up and steady enough that she didn't lose her balance, Caitlyn lowered her head even farther and licked at his balls. They drew up as she laved them with her tongue.

"That's it. Lick them just like that. Aw, hell."

Brody chose that moment to enter her with his hard cock. It pushed through delicate tissues in one hard thrust. Caitlyn screamed around Lamar's dick that was lodged deep in her throat. The pleasure-pain of Brody's entrance sent tingles down to her toes. She backed off of Lamar's cock and looked over her shoulder at Brody. His head was thrown back and his eyes closed with a fierce-looking grimace that looked almost like pain etched on his face. She turned back to Lamar and took him in her mouth again.

"Fuck, you're tight, Caity. I want to bury myself all the way inside of you, but I'm not sure I can squeeze inside of your tight cunt."

She grunted around Lamar's dick and continued bobbing up and down on him. She knew that if Brody started to really pummel her, she'd have to stop sucking on Lamar for fear that it would choke her. Making him come and come soon seemed her only course of action. She increased her suction and used her teeth to rake along the huge vein running the length of his dick. He began thrusting upwards to meet her downward plunges.

Brody slowly began to fuck her until he was able to bury almost all of his long cock inside of her cunt before hitting her cervix. He bumped against it the first time but backed off the second time. Caitlyn wasn't having any of that. She liked her cervix bumped. She began to meet his thrusts with her own until the sound of slapping skin and muffled grunts filled the room.

Lamar's movements became erratic as he grew closer to coming. She redoubled her efforts at sending him over using her mouth, teeth, and tongue. He grabbed her head with both hands as he began shooting his cum deep in her throat. She sucked and swallowed all of it she could as he called out her name then collapsed back against the couch. His cum leaked from the corners of her mouth as she licked her lips.

"God, baby. That was un-fucking-believable," he finally managed after a few seconds of panting.

Brody's grasp on her hips grew tighter as he pumped his cock in and out of her pussy, changing his angle so that he dragged over her G-spot with each thrust. She couldn't help but gasp out a hoarse *yes, more*.

Her orgasm rushed in on her. Caitlyn tried to slow it down, but Brody's expert manipulation of her body wouldn't allow it as he stroked inside of her. His fingers dug into her flesh of her hips. She closed her eyes and threw back her head as the first zapping pleasure hit her unexpectedly. The burn grew, singing through her blood and stimulating her cunt into the first throes of her climax.

Brody's rhythm faltered then grew faster as he tunneled in and out of her fluttering pussy. She could feel her cunt squeezing his cock, milking his dick of his cum. He shouted out her name, filling the condom with his cum just as her orgasm hit her full force. She could hear a scream ringing in her ears. Nothing could compare to the pleasure these two men brought her each and every time.

She moaned as the last vestiges of her orgasm sparked through her cunt, causing her to tighten around Brody's softening cock. He grunted and leaned over her, resting his head between her shoulders.

"God, that was so damn good, baby. I don't think I can move."

She wiggled her ass. "You're going to have to. I can't stay like this much longer."

In fact, she began to sink forward as her shaking arms gave out on her. Brody moved off of her and slowly pulled out, patting her ass as he did. Then he left her. He would dispose of the condom and come back. She was hanging over the arm of the couch totally limp. Her feet no longer touched the ground.

Lamar immediately got up from the couch and pulled her off, picking her up and settling her on the couch with him. She rested her head on his shoulder, realizing that she still had her eyes shut.

"Just rest, Caity. When Brody gets back we'll settle you in bed."

"Nope." Brody walked back into the room. "I promised her she wouldn't end up in bed, so she has to rest on the couch until she's ready to go back to work."

"Bed," she moaned out.

Brody chuckled. "Are you changing your mind?"

"I need a nap."

"Baby, it's nearly seven now. If you take a nap, you'll crash and won't get back up. Then you'll probably wake up at the crack of dawn."

"Damn! You're mean, Brody."

"Just rest on me, Caitydid. Then you can get back up and we'll have something for dinner. You'll feel better in a few minutes." Lamar patted her thigh.

Caitlyn grunted and settled more firmly against him. Brody sat down next to her and pulled her feet up in his lap. He massaged them.

It felt so good that she began to drift into sleep. Brody was having none of that. He ran his finger down the bottom of her foot, causing her to yelp.

"That tickles!"

"Wake up then. You don't need to fall asleep."

"I'll get even with you, Brody. You have to sleep sometime."

He had no doubt she would find a way to get back at him, but he didn't mind. Any attention from Caity was worth it. The more time she spent with them, the closer they could bind her to them. He wanted her to feel so attached to them by the time Brian and the others returned that she wouldn't want to move to Austin at all.

Chapter Fifteen

Lamar woke to find Caitlyn turned toward Brody with her ass pressed up against his cock. It felt good. It felt right. He enjoyed it while she was asleep, knowing that when she woke up she would move. He didn't think that Caitlyn was totally comfortable with staying with them yet. They'd made a lot of progress toward winning her over, but one misstated sentence could have it all come tumbling down on them. Brody was known for saying the wrong thing. Lamar could only pray that he would keep his mouth shut for a change.

"What are you thinking so hard about over there?" Brody's voice, made husky by sleep, barely reached his ears.

"Thinking that we've made some progress, but it wouldn't take much for her to change her mind and leave. Just worrying is all, I guess."

"Worried that I won't be able to keep my mouth shut, you mean."

"Well, you have this way of pissing people off, Brody. Doesn't she relax you when she is around?"

Brody seemed to think a minute, absently stroking Caitlyn's hair down the side of her face.

"Yep, I guess you're right, I do. You think I'm going to be the one to screw this all up, don't you."

"I hope not, Brody, but you need to relax more around her. Don't think about the small things so much. They'll take care of themselves. Relax around her. Let her see you like I do. You're a very dependable, warm-hearted man under all that gruff, and always willing to help someone in need."

Brody shifted uncomfortably in the bed. Caitlyn moaned and turned in the bed, but instead of waking up, she settled back down sans covers, exposing her delicate white mounds with delicate pink flowers standing up on top.

"You make me sound like a saint like that, and we both know I'm no saint in anything I do. So drop the subject."

Between them, Caitlyn squirmed then pushed against each of them as she slowly woke up stretching.

"Drop what subject?" she asked, curiosity getting the better of her despite being only half awake.

"Nothing, baby. Just some stuff at work." Lamar wrapped his arm around her waist and pulled her back against his body.

She wiggled her ass against his hardened dick, and he groaned. He slipped his fingers down her belly to the top of her mound.

"You're being naughty, Caitydid."

"Mmm, really? I thought I was hinting that I was horny."

"Sounds like she knows what she wants, Lamar. Think you should oblige the lady before she changes her mind." Brody rolled over and sat up on the side of the bed.

Lamar felt Caitlyn pull away from him as she sat up on her knees and wrapped her arms around Brody's shoulders. Lamar knew what she was going to say, but he had no idea what to expect from his brother. "Brody, don't go. I want you both. I want to feel your cock deep inside of me while Lamar fucks my mouth."

"Didn't realize you had such a potty mouth on you."

She pulled back and glared at him. "You should talk. You can't say anything without adding a curse word."

"I'm a man. Men curse when need be." He stood up at the side of the bed, naked but uncaring as he continued. "There isn't a thing I could say to you that wouldn't put a frown on your face right now, because I'm tired, half-asleep, horny, and worried."

"Poor thing, carrying all that weight on your shoulders alone. I'm sure Lamar would be glad to take a little of it from you."

Lamar allowed himself a brief smile. She had held her own with his brother. Granted, she hadn't won, but she had settled him down some. He wanted to bet that Brody would stay with them in bed. He would probably grumble, but he would enjoy it just as much as Lamar would. He guessed he was going to owe Caitlyn.

Sure enough, the big man didn't get up, but leaned back in the bed with his hands thrown back behind his head. He grinned over at Lamar.

"Get ready, man. She's going to suck both our dicks together. Then I'll fuck her pretty pussy while she finishes you off. How does that sound to you?"

Lamar thought that sounded pretty damn good to him, but he wondered how she would feel about it? Would she eventually balk at being told what she was going to do? Lamar was afraid so. No matter how a woman was treated, she would eventually want to take over or at the very least, pull back.

Lamar figured the best thing to do at that moment would be to back off and let Brody take over. It would lessen the stress for all of them. Then, if Caity complained or wanted to stop, he'd step in. They had made too much progress to ruin it all in a morning.

"Lamar?" Caity asked, watching him.

"Yeah, baby. Suck my cock real good." He turned in the bed so that he was lying on his back next to Brody.

Caitlyn crawled up their bodies and grasped both dicks in her hands. Then she bent over and drew Brody's hardened cock into her mouth. She sucked her way down the stalk as far as she could go. She held there for several seconds before backing off of him. Turning to Lamar, she did the same thing, but Lamar felt her swallow around him when he was as far down her throat as he could get. The feel of her throat muscles contracting around him was almost as good as her cunt muscles tightening down on his cock when he was balls deep inside of her.

"God, yes, Caity. Harder."

She tightened her grip at the base of his dick and sucked harder as she came back up until she let go of his cockhead with a resounding *pop*. He groaned at the exquisite feel of her mouth on him before she left him needing and pulled off of him. He glanced over at his brother and Caitlyn was just about to suck his dick. Brody held her head steady as she lowered her mouth over his cock. When she had reached the back of her throat, she adjusted her position and somehow managed to go even farther.

Lamar watched as his brother threw back his head and yelled out.

"Hell, yeah!"

The big man grasped her hair in his hand and pumped his cock into her mouth several times before she pulled back and lifted an eyebrow at him as she squeezed his dick with her hand.

"If you can't behave, then keep your hands off my head."

"Fuck, baby. I need to hold you when you're deep-throating me. I can't help it."

"That's fine, Brody, but you were face-fucking me while you were holding me down. Letting you touch me at all was hard to do. The other scared me. I don't like being held down."

"Okay, Brody. We can try it again." She leaned forward as if to take him in her mouth. Brody grasped her shoulders and lightly pushed her back to the bed. He came over her, planting one hand on either side of her head.

"I can't wait to get inside of you, Caitlyn. I want to feel your pussy lips suck me in. I want to watch you eat Lamar's dick. Are you going to do that for me, baby?" He rubbed over her forehead before settling down to screw her.

Lamar watched while holding his breath that Caity would balk at his brother's roughness. When she didn't complain or pull away, he began to have hope that they could convince her that they could take care of her and tend to all her needs. He especially wanted her to consider letting him fuck her tight ass. He knew he was thicker than Brody. Still, he'd had anal sex with other women before. They hadn't complained. If she wouldn't let him, then he would forget it. Making her happy and keeping her there with them was the most important thing. He'd do just about anything to change her mind about staying in Riverbend.

* * * *

Caitlyn could tell that Lamar was nervous about how she would handle Brody's roughness. For the most part, she liked things a little rough, but not painful. Brody had gotten close to her no-fly zone, and she had to do something about it. She hoped he would remember that and not try her like that again. She didn't mind a little force, but he'd been too rough this morning.

She turned over on her back and stared up into Lamar's eyes as he got ready to let her suck his cock. He knelt next to her head and brushed the head of his dick against her lips. She smiled and opened them just far enough to let her questing tongue reach for him. She flicked out her tongue and licked him across the top of his cockhead and over the slit. He hissed out a breath. A single drop of pre-cum emerged from the little slit.

"Aw, hell! That's it, baby. Lick it for me."

She ran the tip of her tongue around his cock then slipped it across the slit and lapped up the tangy little pearl. She sucked on the coronal ring around his cock, using her tongue to tease it as she did. He grabbed her shoulders but didn't try to stop her or control her. He used her for support. She smiled. She liked being able to take care of him.

Brody's big hands spread her legs so that she was totally exposed to his gaze. Her wet pussy would be glittering in the light. She relaxed her thighs and let her legs flop back so that there was more room between them. Then Brody was there, fitting his sheathed cock at her opening. She looked up at him as he leaned on one hand while feeding his hard-as-nails cock into her pussy. He wasn't as thick as

Lamar, but he was longer, and she knew that he would bump her cervix once he got going.

"I'm going to fill you so full of my dick that you won't be able to think of anything else."

He pumped in and out of her in long slow slides as he slowly increased the depth and then the speed. By the time she had Lamar ready to climax, Brody was thrusting in and out of her cunt, grazing her sweet spot with each pass of his cock.

"Aw, hell, baby. I love your mouth." Lamar tugged on her hair as she swallowed around him when he was as deep in her throat as she could comfortably take him.

She used her teeth on the way back up then sucked him down again. She continued over and over until he grasped the top of the headboard, his knuckles turning white as he pumped his cum down her throat in fast, hot spurts. He yelled out her name and then grasped her head, massaging it until she backed off of him, trailing his cum from the corners of her mouth.

"I'd keep your cock away from her mouth now, Lamar. I've been holding back until you were finished so she wouldn't bite it off." Brody readjusted his stance and lifted her bottom off the bed with her legs over his arms.

"Caitlyn, baby. I think you're in for it." Lamar panted as he spoke.

She couldn't say anything because at that moment, Brody slammed into her with the full length of his long cock. She yelped at the sudden attack to her cervix but then hummed her approval as it turned into pleasure. He backed off a little with the next thrust, and she reached up to run her hands up his abdomen to his chest. She loved the light roughness from the sparse chest hair. He leaned farther over her so that she could reach more of him.

"If you have the ability to play with my chest, I'm not doing something right." Brody grunted as he pulled out.

"What are you doing?" She panicked that he was going to just stop fucking her.

"Turning you over so I can get to you better."

He positioned her on her hands and knees, and then he gently pushed against her back until her face was on the covers. She dug her fingers into the soft comforter and spread her legs to give herself some traction.

"Damn, your ass looks good from back here. Lamar, come look at her pussy. It's all pink and wet."

"Look," Lamar said. "She's dripping juice down her leg."

"Please, Brody. Fuck me. I need you in me."

"Easy, Caitydid. I'll take care of you. I'll always take care of you." He pushed his rigid dick deep into her pussy as he reassured her.

She sighed and curled her toes when he pulled out and thrust in once again. Each time he bumped up against her cervix, she felt her orgasm growing. Heat burned along her spine and through her bloodstream. Her body began to tingle all over as she slowly climbed upward toward her peak.

Brody slapped her ass cheek on one side then again on the other. The sweet sting added to the general burn that seemed to permeate every cell of her body. The more he spanked her, the hotter the fire grew. Then he reached around beneath her and ran his finger through her pussy from where they were joined to her clit.

"Ah! God, yes. Please touch me there."

"Not yet, Caity. Not yet."

"I can't stand it. I need to come, Brody. Please!" She knew she was begging, but she couldn't help it.

The pleasure was just out of reach. Even with him hitting her cervix and spanking her ass, she wasn't quite there. It was as if he knew just how much he could torment her without sending her into orgasm. He played her like an expensive instrument until she was begging and then cursing him.

He began rotating his hips with each thrust so that he hit her G-spot. The growing potential of unbelievable pleasure expanded even more and she began to fear it, feared that it would be more than she could handle. Now her body fought to resist the temptation to fly into her climax. She would never survive such an explosion as the one on the horizon appeared to be. She couldn't believe that Brody was tormenting her like this. Surely he realized that it was too much for her to handle.

Still, he didn't slow down or stop his stimulation of her body as his measured thrusts lost their rhythm. He growled at her then reached around her to locate her clit.

"You're going to come before I do."

Brody pinched her clit as he slammed into her, bumping against her cervix once more. She screamed out as pain and pleasure morphed into ecstasy and the promise of something more. She felt her entire body contract as she shot up, up into the sky without a parachute. Surely she would die when she made it back down.

Instead, she slowly floated back down along with birds and butterflies and energy. Then she felt Brody spasm inside her as he thrust one last time before emptying his cum into the condom. She could still feel the scalding hot seed as it filled the condom to capacity. He collapsed over her without a thought to his weight, she was sure. Then Lamar crawled over to them and slapped his brother upside the head.

"You're squishing her, Brody. Hell, you're probably suffocating her." He pulled on his brother's arm and finally got Brody off of her. He rolled over to the side, his cock pulling loose from her with a soggy pop.

"Fuck, the condom." He reached back and pulled it from her where it had come off. Then he climbed off the bed and padded to the bathroom. He returned a few seconds later with a warm bath cloth and cleaned her up.

"I'm not sure, but I think I caught it before any leaked out."

"I'm not on birth control, Brody. I never thought I could get pregnant before."

"It's okay, baby. We'll take good care of you and the baby if it happens. Don't worry about it."

"That's easy for you to say. You're not the one who carries it around and gives birth." She huffed out a breath and rolled over to her back. Lamar was on one side with Brody on the other.

"I'm not going to worry about it because it probably won't happen. It's a one-in-a-million chance."

"Yeah," Lamar said. "It only takes that one time to do the trick, though."

Chapter Sixteen

Brody thought about the possibility of a baby all day as they worked in their shop. He couldn't get it out of his head that he might be a father. Hell, he and Lamar would be great fathers. He hadn't approached Lamar to see what he thought about it. He was sure his brother would be fine with a baby, but he hadn't wanted to broach the subject yet.

What if she really were pregnant and still decided to move to Austin? What would they do? She would be taking their baby with her. He frowned.

"What are you scowling about over there?" Lamar pulled off his helmet and stared at him.

"Just thinking too hard."

"Are you worrying about her being pregnant? 'Cause if you are, get over it. It wasn't her fault. It was ours because we weren't careful."

"I'm not going to blame her. I'm not even upset about it. I'm just thinking that it would mean a lot of changes in all of our lives. I take it you're happy about the possibility."

"I wouldn't be upset if she turned up pregnant, but I hope it doesn't happen. She would have too much to deal with at one time. Between being pregnant and moving from Mississippi and starting a new business…"

"You're assuming she is going to stay here with us." Brody interrupted him.

Lamar winced and looked away. "Yeah. I guess I'm not letting myself believe otherwise. I can't imagine living without her, Brody."

"I know what you mean. But we have to face facts. She might not stay with us. We still have time to convince her, but if she ends up pregnant, we might have trouble."

He watched his brother's shoulders sink. He guessed Lamar had told himself that it was a done deal. She was with them now and would be from now on. Brody had known better than to let his hopes get up. He shored up his heart once again, because he knew that more than likely, she wouldn't stay there in Riverbend.

Brody finished the length of pipe he was working on and decided to take a break. He needed some coffee. Neither he nor Lamar had gotten much sleep the night before. Neither had Caitlyn for that matter. He grinned. She had seemed to be walking a little slowly that morning. He figured she would be a bit sore. They would need to go easy on her tonight.

Call her, Brody. Ask her how she's feeling. He shook his head to rid himself of the thought. That was more along the lines of what Lamar would do. He pursed his lips and called Lamar over to the office.

"What?" Lamar called back but didn't stop what he was doing.

"Come here. I have something for you to do."

Lamar sighed and dropped the length of pipe he was machining to fit something. When he walked up to the office, Brody handed him a cup of coffee. Lamar took a sip before he lifted an eyebrow with a questioning look aimed Brody's way.

"I thought you might call Caity and see how she's doing this morning. We had her up late last night and I noticed she seemed like she was a little sore. You know, between the legs." Brody stood back so that his brother could reach the phone.

"Why me?"

"You're better at that sort of stuff than I am. I'm liable to hurt her feelings or say something out of line."

"You're right about that." Lamar sighed and reached over to grab the phone.

"Put it on speakerphone so I can hear."

"Fine." Lamar pushed the button to turn it on then dialed the store where she was working on the mail-order business for the day. Brody watched each button as he pushed it.

Then the phone rang. Brody closed his eyes and imagined her hurrying from the front of the store to the back where the phone was located. They hadn't hooked up one in the front part yet. They needed to think about doing that in the near future. Something could happen while she was up front and not able to get to the back. Right now, he was more interested in hearing her voice answer the phone.

"Um, hello?" She sounded winded. He had been right. She'd had to run to catch the phone. He hoped she didn't knock anything off and break it. She would feel obligated to pay for it, and he knew she was on a limited budget.

"Hey, Caity. It's Lamar. How are you feeling? Are you about finished?"

"I'm fine. Just really busy, is all."

"There weren't but about three packages to wrap when we looked yesterday," Lamar said.

"Just three? They sure multiplied overnight." She huffed out a breath. "I've just packed up my fifth box for the afternoon. I'll take them to the post office around four so I don't have to come back if I don't want to. It's usually only one or two days a week."

"I didn't think there were but a few each week." Lamar looked over at Brody and shrugged.

"Yeah, well, people have been busy buying evidently. The store isn't even officially open, and I keep getting people stopping by and pointing at stuff in the window and slip their information under the door for me to find and fill their order. I guarantee you that they will show up at quitting time to get their gifts."

Brody could hear the laughter in her voice. She wasn't really fussing. She enjoyed it. Plus, she got to play with some of the items as well. The Southworths' store catered to an eclectic group of people.

Lamar and Brody both would be going there a lot more in the future. They sold adult-themed gifts. Brian and Andy were running the mail-order business, leaving the store and its sexy-looking underwear for her to deal with.

"Hey, sexy." Brody smiled, knowing she was scowling across the phone line. Instead of telling him to stop calling her that, she sighed.

"Hey, Brody. How are you and Lamar doing?"

"Lamar is right here, baby. Doing fine. Wishing you were here, though."

Brody shook his head. "How are you feeling after all of our, um activity last night and this morning?"

The other side of the phone line was deathly quiet for a few seconds. Then Caitlyn spoke up a little clearer than before.

"I'm fine. Maybe a little sore, but nothing that won't heal. Why?" Brody could hear the caution in her question. "Because I know how to apply a Band-Aid, take ibuprofen when I need to, and how to say no, if I need to."

"Don't mind him, Caity." Lamar pulled the phone closer to him. "Do you need help with the post office this morning? It sounds like you have a lot to mail."

"It's all small stuff. I can handle it. I'll let you know if I get anything large. I'm not going to try and carry something big if I can help it. So don't worry that I won't ask, because I will."

"Good girl." Brody couldn't help but chime in.

"I'm not talking to you right now."

Lamar chuckled and punched him on the shoulder. Brody grinned. He knew she was kidding.

"I need to go, you two. I'll see you at dinner tonight."

"Call us if you need us."

"Bye, guys." The phone went dead with a click.

"Do you think she sounds a little friendlier toward us?" Brody asked after a few seconds.

"I don't know. She's always been friendly. We need to try and convince her to stay here, but I'm afraid to alienate us by bringing it up too much."

"I was thinking the same thing. The more time I spend with her, the greater my chances of saying something to screw it up."

Lamar opened his mouth to say something, and Brody had a feeling he knew what it was.

"Don't even say it, because I'm not going to stay away from her."

"It was just a thought. You're the one who said you couldn't keep your mouth shut."

Brody shook his head and went back to working on the section of pipe he was trying to fit. Somehow, he had to figure out a way to convince her to stay. If she turned out to be pregnant, he might have a better chance, but she would always feel pressured into it for the baby's sake. He didn't really want her to feel like she didn't have a choice. He wanted her to have the choice and still choose them. He wanted them to be the life she chose for herself.

* * * *

Caitlyn locked up the store at the end of the week, tired but satisfied. Her brother's business was growing already and they hadn't even advertised nor had a grand opening. She was selling from their inventory both by mail from their webpage and to walk-ins who wanted to look around. She didn't have the heart to tell them no when they wanted to buy something.

She had even given a few of the older women of the town a tour of the store. Each of the four women had bought something. She was sure Brian would fuss when they got back, but he'd see the bank account and change his tune awful fast. She hoped she had ordered the right things from their distributor and that they would come in soon. The inventory was getting pretty low.

Checking the lock, she picked up her satchel and turned to head out to her SUV. She couldn't wait to get in the shower when she got to the guys' house. When she drew closer to the vehicle, there was a man leaning against her car door. She slowed up and stopped a few feet away.

"Can I help you?"

"You're the young lady living with Brody and Lamar, right?"

"That's right." She cringed inside. Was he going to tell her what a whore she was? She started to turn around to go back inside the store.

Someone walked up behind her, crowding close to her. She could smell body odor and didn't want to turn to see who it was. Instead, she stiffened, biting her lower lip.

The other man pushed off of the SUV and walked toward her. She had nowhere to go. He stopped right in front of her so that she could see his eyes were brown and smell his breath. He'd had something with garlic earlier. The odor wafted by her nose just before he reached out and wrapped his hand around her neck and squeezed.

"Listen to me very closely. I want you to take a message back to them for me. Understand?"

She nodded her head the best she could.

"They need to step away from government contracting jobs. They need to be happy with what they've got and stop horning in on my territory, namely, national, state, county, and city government jobs. I want them to drop this latest contract they've picked up from the state, and you're going to convince them to do it for me."

"Why do you think they will listen to me?"

"Because they are good guys and wouldn't like for anything to happen to you."

Caitlyn's insides froze as the insinuation that something might happen to her sank in. He was threatening her. She was tired of being used by people. She jerked free of the man's hand.

"You can tell them yourself. I'm not a damn message system. Move out of my way."

He stared at her for a few seconds then nodded his head and stepped away from the door of the SUV. The man behind her didn't grab her either. She lifted her chin and pushed the little button on her key fob to unlock the door. Then she walked toward it and reached out to the handle. Suddenly the side of her face was slammed against the window and someone whispered into her ear.

"Tell them before something more serious happens to you—or them." The hand pressed harder for a few seconds then released the pressure.

She stood there trying to catch her breath for a few seconds before turning around and finding there was no one there. She fought down the panic that threatened to overwhelm her. She felt something trickle down her face and realized it was blood—her blood. She reached up and found a small knot growing above her eyebrow. Her hand came away with blood on it, shaking as she looked at it. She swallowed hard and wiped the blood on her jeans. Then she climbed into the car and after closing and locking the door, grabbed a handful of tissues to staunch the bleeding.

Caitlyn didn't know what to do. She caught her reflection in the rearview mirror and realized two things. One, she looked scared, and two, she was going to have a black eye by the looks of it. Her cheek was already darkening.

What was she going to do? She knew if the guys saw her they would be upset. Then when she told them what the bastard had said, they would blame themselves. She ran a shaking hand over the unharmed side of her face and tried to think. What if she moved out and back into Brian's house? Would that help? She doubted it. The guys would come get her and then see her injured face. It wouldn't thwart the stranger from using her anyway.

The ringing of her cell phone interrupted her thoughts. She looked at the display and sighed. It was Lamar. She didn't answer it. She could tell him that she had been driving and couldn't answer it. It bought her a little time, but no matter how hard she thought, she couldn't come up with an answer to her dilemma.

Caitlyn pulled the tissues away from her aching head and was relieved to see that it had stopped bleeding. She surveyed herself and found that she had smeared blood on her forehead and down her cheek where it had dripped to her T-shirt. Her cheek was bruised and throbbing, and her clothes had blood on them. She could run to the house and clean up, but it wouldn't hide the injuries. Still, it would lessen the shock of them seeing her covered in blood.

Her mind made up, she started the SUV and pulled away from the curb. If the light traffic would cooperate, she should have plenty of time to make it to the house and shower and change clothes before they arrived.

To her dismay, both of their trucks were already parked in the garage. After parking and shutting off the engine, she sat there a few seconds, trying to get up the nerve to go inside. As it was, she didn't have to. Lamar and Brody walked out with grins on their faces. She watched those grins fade to frowns and then to outright rage by the time they reached her.

Brody jerked open the door and pulled her out of the vehicle. Lamar was right there with him. They searched her for further injuries without saying a word. That didn't last long, though.

"What happened? Who did this to you?" Brody demanded.

"Brody, let's get her inside and get some ice on her face."

"Fuck, that's right. I'm sorry, baby. How in the hell did this happen?"

"Can I tell you after I get something for a headache?"

Lamar hurried ahead of them. By the time they made it inside, he had a glass of water and two pain pills for her in the living room. He returned a few seconds later with a bath cloth and began cleaning her hands and dabbing at the blood on her face with a gentle touch. Brody was vibrating with anger but waited while his brother took care of her.

"Tell me what happened."

"I locked up the store and walked over to my car, but there was a man leaning on the door. I started to go back to the store, but someone else walked up behind me and kept me from moving. Then the first guy came over and put his hand around my throat. He threatened me."

"Why? What did he say?" Lamar had finished cleaning her face and was holding a bag of ice to the side of her face.

"He said to tell you to stay away from government jobs. They were his domain, and you were getting in his way. You're supposed to drop the state one you have now."

"Or what?" Brody's expression looked sick to her.

"He said you would do it because you wouldn't want anything to happen to me." She ended in a near whisper. Her voice had grown hoarse.

"Fuck!" Brody started to punch the wall, but Lamar stopped him.

"Don't do it. You might break your hand and we'll need that hand later."

Brody pulled away from him and turned back to Caitlyn. He gently cupped her face. Then he kissed her other cheek and wrapped his arms around her waist.

"Baby, I'm so sorry. I'll get him. He won't hurt you again. I promise."

Chapter Seventeen

"Lamar, call Sheriff Tidwell. As much as I want to break that guy's neck with my own two hands, we've got to follow the rules." Brody wanted to pound out his anger on the man's face but knew that wasn't the way to go.

"Do you know who he is?" Caitlyn's hands held a slight tremor as she held the bag of ice to her cheek.

"No. We've been having some problems but didn't know who was responsible. I think we can find out now that we know why they are fucking with us."

Lamar walked back over to them, holding the phone to his chest.

"He wants us to come down to the station and fill out a report. He's going to personally handle the paperwork."

"Why can't he come out here?"

"His secretary is gone for the day and the other deputies are all out on calls. Someone has to man the phones in the meantime." Lamar shrugged.

"Okay. Tell him we'll be there in a few minutes." Brody pulled Caitlyn into his arms and held her.

He hated knowing that she was hurting, and the fact that it was because of them made it even harder to swallow. They were supposed to keep their woman safe, not be the reason behind her getting beat up. Anger washed through his veins like venom. He glanced over at Lamar and could tell his brother was just as pissed. You didn't expect something like this in Riverbend. For the most part, it was a quiet little town where everyone looked out for everyone else. Lately there had been some unusual activities that had everyone a little on edge, but the sheriff had kept things on an even keel. Now this had happened.

"Caity, do you feel like going and talking to the sheriff? He's a good man."

"I need to tell him while it's still fresh in my head. If I wait, I might forget something important. I want him caught before he can do anything to your business."

"Forget about the business," Lamar began. "All we are worried about is you. Anyone who would threaten a woman will cause trouble for everyone and won't have a sense of fair play. He could change his mind and come after you anyway. I want him caught."

"That goes double for me." Brody slowly released her from his grip and checked her face once again. "Let's go so we can get you settled down for the evening."

Lamar held the door for her as they filed out of the house. Brody didn't let her any farther than arm's reach from him until they got to the truck, then he let Lamar take over and get her settled inside. Once they were all loaded up, Brody drove them back into town toward the sheriff's office. He paid close attention to Caitlyn, worried that she might have a slight concussion and second-guessing himself about making her go to the hospital to be evaluated.

After parking, Lamar helped Caitlyn down. He walked around the truck to join them as they headed up the walkway toward the front door of the sheriff's office.

It was cool inside compared to the heat still lingering outside. Brody checked his watch and found that it was already approaching seven. The sheriff was working late. He had a wife at home waiting on him, too. Beth was a pretty little thing who edited romance books. Sheriff Tidwell and his brother were married to her.

When they didn't see anyone in the front part of the office, Brody led them toward the back where the sound of a voice led them to the sheriff's office. The blinds were open, but the door was closed. The sheriff sat leaned back in his desk chair with one hand thrown over his eyes talking to someone about something to do with a bail skipper and the need to be more aware of where their parolees were at all times.

He finally moved his hand after squeezing the bridge of his nose and looked up. He stared right though Caitlyn and into Brody's face. Then he stood up and quickly wrapped the call up. Tidwell was across the room in two long strides. He opened the door and held out his hand to greet them.

"I'm Mack Tidwell. Pleased to meet you, ma'am." They shook hands, and he turned to greet both Brody and Lamar. "Let's get settled and we can get to the bottom of the problem. Do you want coffee or a soft drink?" After everyone settled down in a chair, he sat back behind the desk and pulled out a folder.

Brody could tell Caity was nervous by the way she clasped and unclasped her hands in her lap. She kept her gaze averted from the sheriff's as if she were ashamed of the way she looked with the beginnings of a knot on her head and the blossoming bruise.

"Ma'am, I'm sorry this happened to you in Riverbend. We try to keep this place as safe as possible to assure families they can live here without being harassed or shot at."

"I haven't been shot at yet."

"I don't trust that it won't be next, though." The sheriff opened the folder and pulled out a form.

He fed it in the printer then pulled up a program on his computer. He typed in a few commands, and then he started asking about getting up and who left first. By the time they got to what actually happened after work, she was much more relaxed and was able to walk through it again with a good bit of detail that he pulled from her. It amazed her when he read it back to her just how much she had remembered.

"Does that sound about right?"

"Yes, it sounds exactly right. I can't believe how much I actually remembered. I'm sorry I didn't see the other man to give you a description of him."

"You've given me plenty to work with. We'll get to the bottom of this. In the meantime, you don't need to be alone at any time. Someone has to be with you. I don't trust this guy to play by the rules that he's set."

Brody had already come to that conclusion. They would take turns staying with her at the store when she had to be there and keep her at the shop with them when she didn't.

"Are you planning to drop the state project he was talking about?" the sheriff asked Brody.

"As long as we can keep Caitlyn safe I don't plan on giving in to the bastard. What do you suggest?"

"Play it normal with the exception of keeping her with you at all times. I'm going to work from this end at finding out who he is and everything I can on him. You keep Caitlyn safe and call me if he shows up or makes a move."

Brody felt Caitlyn stiffen next to him. She shouldn't have to worry about someone wanting to hurt her. He never dreamed anyone would ever give a rat's ass about what he and Lamar did. They were machinists, for heaven's sake. They weren't politicians or bankers or some bigwigs. The entire town would be at risk as long as this guy and his goons were around.

Sheriff Tidwell closed the folder after adding a few pages from the printer to the small stack. Then he stood up and escorted them to the front of the building. There he opened the door and reminded them to call him if anything happened or the man showed up again.

Lamar helped her up into the truck as Brody climbed into the driver's side. The sheriff had warned him that it sounded like they were dealing with a small town's version of the mafia or that one of the bigger families had moved deeper into the west. He personally didn't see a family like that paying attention to the small community of Riverbend. No, the bastard was some wannabe gang leader of some kind. Tidwell would get to the bottom of it. If not, Brody was willing to step in and handle it himself. No one was going to hurt Caitlyn again.

* * * *

The numbness had worn off by the time they had returned from the sheriff's office. Now Caitlyn was shaking all over and couldn't get warm. Her face ached as did her head despite the painkillers she'd taken earlier. It was too soon for more. She needed to calm down, because it was upsetting the men to see her like that.

Brody fixed them something to eat while Lamar held her on the couch. He'd wrapped her in a blanket in an effort to warm her up and stop the shaking. A blanket wasn't going to warm her when it was her bones that had gone cold. It would take something else to eradicate the gut-wrenching cold that had settled there at the realization that she could have been killed.

Somehow, it hadn't really dawned on her until they were at the sheriff's office that she was lucky to be alive. She had a lot to be thankful for. When everything was over, she planned to sit down and count her blessings. It had made her realize that life was short and she needed to take every opportunity she had to enjoy it.

They ate in silence, each in their own thoughts. Brody's brooding stare off into nothing worried her more than Lamar's quiet contemplation of the situation. All she could think about was the many different ways there were to die based on her knowledge of old movies about the mob.

Finally, she snapped out of it, realizing that by letting it paralyze her, she was feeding the men's anger. They needed to calm down, and she needed to think logically. She stood up to carry her plate to the sink. As long as she stayed with the men, nothing would happen to her. She had faith that they would protect her. The enormity of that realization hit her, and she sat back down with a plop. They really did care about her that strongly. Did that mean love?

"Caity? Are you okay?" Lamar reached over and took her hand.

"I'm fine. I just got up too fast and got a little dizzy."

"We should have taken you to the hospital and let them check you out." Brody turned her to face him.

"No, really, guys. I'm fine." She pulled away from Brody and stood up slower this time before carrying her plate to the sink.

"I think I'm going to take a bath and go to bed early. I'm tired."

"I'll run your bathwater for you, baby." Lamar stacked his and Brody's plates on top of hers.

"Thanks, I appreciate it." She hugged Lamar then slipped out of his arms and slid into Brody's.

She could tell he was surprised by that. More than likely, he thought she blamed him for the attack. She couldn't blame him any more than she could blame Lamar. She wasn't sure why she needed to feel his arms around her unless it was because she was in love with them and was tired of fighting it. Sure, she would be leaving soon, but until then, she could enjoy the warmth of the two men. She had been honest with them about leaving. She still felt like it was the right thing to do.

Now she wondered if they were in love with her. They hadn't said so in as many words, but their actions pointed toward it. How did she feel about that? Did it change anything? Caitlyn followed Lamar up the stairs to the bedroom. She pulled off her clothes, tossing them in a pile to be washed. When she walked into the bathroom, it was to find Lamar turning the water off.

"Your bath awaits you, my lady." He grinned and then let his hungry eyes roam down her body.

She felt her face heat at his obvious perusal of her body. When he looked back into her eyes, his had darkened with desire. Then they rested on her blackened eye and he winced.

"That really looks like it hurts. I'm sorry, Caity."

"Wasn't yours or Brody's fault. It will go away soon."

"Not soon enough. It just never entered our minds that someone would deliberately hurt you. Not in Riverbend."

"It's done now. Let's drop it." She didn't want them dwelling on it even though she knew the sight of her bruised face would keep it fresh in their memories.

"Better get into the tub before the water turns cold." Lamar held out his hand to help her step into the tub.

She took his hand and let him help. She carefully knelt then sat back into the wonderfully warm water. It was just this side of scalding. Closing her eyes, she let the sensation of drifting help her relax. She knew when Lamar left because of the slight breeze that floated across her face when he closed the door. Other than that, she felt nothing but the steaming hot water as it soothed away some of her tenseness.

After a while, the water began to cool. She debated adding more hot water and staying a little longer, but decided she would end up falling asleep in the tub if she did. That would earn her wet hair and a nose full of water. Lamar had left a towel out for her, so she quickly dried off and let the water out of the tub. When she turned around to head toward the bedroom, she caught a glimpse of her reflection in the mirror.

The purplish bruise around her eye was heaviest on her cheekbone. She also had a nasty looking cut and bruise on her forehead just above her eyebrow. She really was lucky they hadn't hurt her worse. There hadn't been anyone around when she walked out to her SUV. She made a face at herself in the mirror and turned off the light.

She was surprised to see both Lamar and Brody sitting on the edge of the bed waiting on her. They had stripped, and she realized they were going to go to bed with her so she wouldn't be alone. As sleepy as she was, she doubted she would have been scared, but she wasn't going to say anything. She would feel better cuddled between them.

Lamar climbed in and scooted over to the other side. Brody kissed her lightly on the lips and helped her up before slipping into the bed next to her. He pulled up the covers as she curled up around Lamar. With the bruises being on her left side, she had to lay on her right. That meant Lamar was her pillow and Brody would keep her ass warm. Just knowing that they were there for her would help keep the dreams away.

"Are you comfortable, Caity?" Brody's warm breath tickled her ear.

"I'm good. I've got the best pillow and butt warmer in the world."

"Somehow I'm not offended by that."

"Go to sleep, Caity," Lamar said with a yawn.

She almost said I love you as she drifted off, but she caught herself. She couldn't tell them and then leave them. Did she really have to leave them?

Chapter Eighteen

Caitlyn looked over her shoulder at where Lamar was sitting in the back of the store. He was reading a trade magazine while she finished printing off labels to package up the sales from the website for mailing. There were only two things today. She was glad. Her arms were sore from wrapping and boxing up the six from the day before.

Despite her tender muscles, she was a little less stressed having found out that she wasn't pregnant. Even though a part of her had almost wished that it were true, she knew it was for the best. She had too much going on in her life right now to handle being pregnant. It would have further complicated an already complicated situation. The men had taken the news in stride though she thought Lamar might have been a little disappointed.

"Sure you don't need any help with that?" Lamar had looked up from the magazine and was watching her.

"Thanks, but I've got it. There's only two today. Nothing like yesterday."

"Anything big?"

"Nope, all small. Lucked out today." She grinned then winced. Her face was still sore, even after four days.

He nodded and went back to reading. She stood up and carried her labels to the wrapping table and began pulling together the items she would be shipping out. Once she had them packaged up and labeled, Caitlyn walked over to Lamar and wrapped her arms around him from behind.

"All finished, Caity?"

"Ready to go to the post office."

"We'll grab lunch and then head over to the shop. Anything you want to grab to take with you?"

"I've got my book. I'll be fine."

Lamar handed her the magazine before grabbing the box holding the items to be mailed. He checked the area before nodding that it was okay for her to leave the store. He waited while she locked up and then they hurried to the truck. Every time she had made this walk in the last few days, her heart sped up and the palms of her hands grew sweaty. So far, nothing more had happened.

They drove to the post office and quickly mailed the packages. Then Lamar drove them to the diner. Caitlyn wasn't really hungry but figured she needed to eat something. Finally, she settled on a ham and cheese sandwich. Lamar ordered the lunch special of fried chicken and mashed potatoes.

Mattie, the diner's owner, delivered them herself.

"Hey, Lamar, Caity. How are you two doing? How's Brody?"

"We're all fine. How are Nate and Bruce?"

"They're fine. Bruce said there was someone he didn't recognize filling up at the gas station when he drove in to work today. He called the sheriff and let him know the details."

"Tell him I said thanks, Mattie. Can't be too careful nowadays."

"Caitlyn, do you need anything?" Mattie squeezed her shoulder.

"No, thanks, Mattie. I'm fine. The guys pretty much take care of everything."

"They better. They don't want the town coming down on them for neglecting you."

Caitlyn started to laugh, but saw that Mattie was serious. That realization caught her off guard. Not only did the people of Riverbend accept the unusual lifestyles of the citizens living there, they supported the people living there and looked out for each other. It was a sobering thought.

They finished their meal, and after getting a hamburger and fries to go for Brody, they headed toward the shop. Lamar was silent the entire ride there. She held the take-out bag in her lap along with her book. When they pulled up outside their place of business, Lamar had her stay in the truck until he could come around and help her down.

"You handle the food and your stuff. I'll get all the doors."

She let him help her down from the truck and then hurried over to the door where Brody held it open for them to come in.

"Any trouble?" he asked as she handed him his hamburger.

"None. Didn't even see a tail. Bruce saw someone new in town and called Tidwell to tell him about it. Figured we should call and find out the details on what to be watching for."

Brody nodded and took a bite out of his burger.

"I'm going to go sit in the office and read." Caitlyn accepted the quick kiss from Lamar and the pat on the ass from Brody.

She closed the door behind her and sank into the barely comfortable office chair. After squirming around for a few seconds, she finally accepted that it wasn't going to get any better and opened her book. The story finally sucked her in and she forgot all about the uncomfortable chair.

Several hours later, Brody opened the office door, startling her into losing her place in the book. She nearly jumped out of the chair and scowled at him.

"Sorry. I'll knock next time to let you know I'm coming in. I was just getting Lamar and me some water. Do you want a bottle?"

"Sure, thanks. What time is it?" She grabbed her purse to check her phone.

"Nearly four. We've got another two hours of work to get done before we can call it a night. Are you okay with that?"

"Sure."

Someone knocked on the outside door. Brody stiffened and stepped between her and the office window looking out over the shop. She peered around him and watched Lamar walk across the floor to answer the door. He stood to one side of the door. She couldn't hear him but saw his mouth move. Then he opened the door and the sheriff and another man entered the shop.

Brody relaxed in front of her and headed for the door. Caitlyn wasn't going to be left out of the loop. She followed behind him as he walked over to where the three men were talking.

"Sheriff. What do you have?" Brody wrapped an arm around her shoulder and kept her close to his side.

"I wanted to fill you in on what I've found out." He turned toward her and smiled. "Ma'am. I'd like you to meet one of my deputies, Jace Vincent. You might see him around some. I have him keeping an eye on you when you're in the area."

She smiled and nodded toward the other man. He nodded back. She was surprised when Lamar moved closer to her and Brody tightened his hold. They were staking their claim of her. It amused her to think that they felt the need to do it.

"So what do you have for us, Sheriff?" Lamar repeated Brody's question.

"So far, there are two companies that have bid on the government project that you have. One is Holston's and the other is Azzali Steele. If I had to guess, I would put my money on Azzali. They have mafia connections and have a large number of government contracts to their name. Most of them are in the San Antonio region."

"I've never heard of the mafia being in Texas before." Lamar shook his head.

The sheriff shrugged. "They haven't really done anything to put them in the spotlight until now. I'm thinking the slowed economy is hurting them like it's hurting all of us."

"You're probably right. How do we handle this?" Brody asked.

"There was a stranger in town today. A tag belonging to Tomas Azzali was spotted on a black Lincoln Town Car getting gas here in town this morning. So far, I haven't been able to find that car anywhere in the area. Either they left Riverbend or they've found somewhere to lay low."

Caitlyn shivered beneath Brody's arm. "So there is a good possibility that the mafia is here and waiting on a chance to get me?"

"Shh, baby. No one's going to get you." Brody scowled at Tidwell.

"I'm going to have one of my men cruise by your house off and on all night tonight to see if they show up. In the meantime, stay together and stay out of the open as much as possible."

"You'll let us know if you learn anything else."

The sheriff nodded and turned toward the outside door. Brody reached out and stopped him with a hand on his arm.

"Sheriff, thanks. I'm a little tense about the entire situation."

"Understood."

He and the deputy left with Lamar locking the door behind them. She wrapped her arms around herself and shivered. Just the thought of them being in the area scared her. She trusted that the guys would keep her safe at the expense of their own safety. That worried her. She didn't want anyone to get hurt.

"Do you want to go back to the office and read? We've still got another couple of hours." Brody rubbed the pad of his thumb over her chin.

"I think I'll sit out here and watch you. It's really kind of interesting. You do a lot of different kind of things. I guess I figured you would just work on machines or something."

"We pretty much deal with anything metal. We did some custom work for a biker gang not long ago. Probably one of the more interesting jobs we've had in a while." Lamar winked at her.

"I bet there were biker babes to watch." Caitlyn smirked at him.

"Well, we were really too busy to do much window-shopping."

"Uh-huh." She shook her head and took a seat on a stool against one of the walls. "I happen to know for a fact that you are very good at multitasking."

He had the grace to blush. She liked that she was able to get to him. Brody, on the other hand, wasn't the least bit affected by her teasing. Instead, he returned to what he had been working on earlier.

Caitlyn remembered that Brody had planned to get water for them earlier. She stood up and hurried to the office, where she retrieved three bottles of water, her book, and her purse. She handed each of them a bottle and then returned to her place by the wall.

Two hours later, Brody called a halt to their work and the three of them locked up and headed back to the house. Relief poured over her when they finally walked in and locked the door behind them. She hadn't realized just how stressed she had been until it lifted.

"I'll cook after I've had a shower." Brady walked across the room, heading toward the stairs.

"I'll cook. You two have been cooking for me ever since I got here. I can cook."

Lamar shrugged and looked at Brody. "Sure. If you want to."

"Good. Go shower and I'll take care of the meal tonight."

She quickly prepared an easy meal that she hoped would fill them up. She liked to cook but usually there had been no one but her to cook for in the past. When Harold had been around, they often went out to eat. It would be easy to get back in the habit of cooking. Realizing where her mind was going, Caitlyn forced herself to think about her brother's business and how surprised he and the others would be when they returned.

Brody and Lamar walked into the kitchen fresh from their showers by the looks of their still-damp hair. She directed them to the table and proceeded to bring the food over. Lamar jumped up to help her despite her assurance that she had it handled.

"It's not much, but it should be filling. Next time I'll plan something ahead of time."

They assured her it was good and proceeded to clean their plates then ask for more. She ended up with no leftovers to put away. She decided that was as close to perfection as she could get.

The men insisted on handling the cleanup since she cooked, leaving her with nothing to do other than watch TV. Somewhere in the middle of a program, she fell asleep and woke up to Brody carrying her upstairs.

"Sorry. I didn't mean to fall asleep like that."

"We could all use an early night. Stress will wear you out like that." Brody walked into the bedroom where Lamar was turning back the covers on the bed.

"Put me down, Brody. I need to take a bath first."

"Want me to run your water for you?"

"Naw, I've got it. Just let me down."

He let her slide down his body until her feet touched the floor. Then he released her with a soft slap on the ass. She smiled at him over her shoulder before walking to the bathroom.

"Don't spend the night in there. Hurry up and come to bed, Caity."

"I won't be long." She closed the door and turned on the water to fill the tub.

As soon as she finished undressing, Caitlyn eased into the tub and quickly washed off. She was tempted to relax for a few minutes but decided she would rather spend the time in bed with Brody and Lamar. After drying off, she opened the bathroom door and hurried across the cool room to climb over Brody and scoot down under the covers between the two men.

"Damn, you're cold." Lamar wrapped himself around her despite his complaint.

"Make sure she's warmed up before she touches me." Brody scooted closer to the edge of the bed.

Caitlyn grinned and reached out and planted her cold feet on his thighs. He yelped then cursed.

"Come here, you little tease." Brody pulled her out of Lamar's arms and rolled her under him. "I'm thinking you're feeling a little neglected, aren't you, Caity." He ran his tongue along her bottom lip before sucking it in and teasing it.

She opened her mouth as soon as he released her lip. He immediately captured her tongue and sucked on it. She moaned when he released it and pulled away.

"Did I hurt you, baby? How's your cheek feel?"

"You didn't hurt me. I'm fine. I want you, Brody. I want to feel you and Lamar as deep as you can get."

"We'll take care of you. Just let us do all the work." Brody rolled off of her before drawing her earlobe into his mouth.

She closed her eyes and enjoyed the sensation of having her earlobe sucked. Then Lamar drew in her nipple to suck and tease as he massaged her other breast with his hand. They licked and caressed every inch of her body from her head to her toes before Brody settled himself between her legs. He looked deep into her eyes as he fisted his sheathed cock. Holding it steady, he slowly entered her wet pussy.

He pulled out and pushed forward again and again until his dick was deep inside her cunt. She savored the fullness along with the tiny bites of pain that Lamar's teeth gave her as he bit each nipple. Each time they took her, Caitlyn felt the screws tighten just a little more on the bindings around her heart. She knew that leaving them would tear it apart.

Brody took her long and slow. Each stroke lifted her higher, each retreat rasped pleasure across her body. Nothing would ever be this good, no one would ever replace what they gave her.

Lamar twisted her nipple just right, and fire bloomed in her veins once again. The familiar burn that ignited all her cells centered in her cunt and lit up her clit so that every sensation was magnified ten times. She didn't think she could go any higher, but each time, they proved her wrong.

Brody thrust into her body harder and faster now, racing toward completion, and Caitlyn was there waiting for him with open arms as they both tumbled head over heels into an ocean of pleasure that continued even as Lamar took Brody's place.

He gave her no time to recover. Instead, he was balls deep inside her pussy in three strokes of his thick dick. Again the pressure grew, and again she fought it as it seemed to overwhelm her. Brody was there at her ear, filling her head with dirty little words that amped up her pleasure until she came, screaming their names.

She was barely aware of Lamar emptying his cum into the condom deep in her cunt. Exhaustion pulled her under even before she felt Lamar leave her body. This time there were no dreams.

Chapter Nineteen

Early Saturday morning, Brody finished up his coffee and waited for the other two to make it downstairs. He had little doubt that Lamar was delaying Caity with sex. He grinned. He'd done the same thing the morning before in the shower. He couldn't get enough of being inside of her. It was the only time he felt like she was all of theirs, the only time he could pretend she wasn't going anywhere.

They would work a half day at the shop and then spend the rest of the day over at Brian's store finishing up orders still waiting to be mailed. They had gotten behind when the orders had suddenly tripled in number.

He walked over to the stairs and yelled at them to hurry up.

"Your breakfast is getting cold and I'm drinking all the coffee."

A few minutes later the sound of footsteps on the stairs let him know they had heard him. When they walked into the kitchen with guilty looks on their faces he could only shake his head.

"Come on, you two. We need to get to work. We've got a long day ahead of us."

"Sorry, Brody. Lamar wouldn't leave me alone to get dressed."

"Don't blame it on me, Caity. You're the one who kept looking at my dick until it was hard as steel. I had to do something, or I'd never have gotten my zipper up."

"Whatever, finish eating and let's head out." Brody poured coffee into two more cups and handed them to Lamar and Caitlyn.

They rushed through breakfast and hurried outside to the truck. Lamar drove, leaving Brody free to tease Caity on the drive in to the shop. By the time they arrived, she was disheveled and panting. He loved seeing her that way, almost as much as he loved to watch her face when she came.

They climbed out of the truck and walked up to the door talking about the TV show they had watched the night before. Out of nowhere, the sound of squealing tires jerked them around to see a black van speed down the street in their direction. Even before it drew even with the shop, the door slid open and hooded men raised guns to pepper the front of the shop with them in the crosshairs.

Brody acted without thinking and shoved Caitlyn to the ground. Even as he dove over her, the sound of bullets popping all around him filled the air. Almost as fast as it started, it was over and the van sped away. The sound of sirens filled the suddenly too-quiet air around them.

He rolled off of Caitlyn and looked around for his brother. Lamar was pulling himself to a sitting position looking around. Brody grabbed Caitlyn by the arms and drew her up and into his arms.

"Fuck, baby. Are you okay?"

"I–I'm not sure. I think so."

"Lamar, you all right?"

"Yeah. What about you?"

"I'm good." He continued to hold Caity in his arms as a sheriff's car pulled into his drive with lights flashing.

"Are you guys all right?" Deputy Jace Vincent called out through the open window of the car.

"We're fine. Did you catch the bastards that tried to kill us?"

"Silas has them at the end of the road. They didn't know the street had a dead end to it."

"Thank God." Caitlyn's shivers were hard enough to sway him standing there.

"Go on inside and lock the door. Wait until one of us comes to take your statements. I need to go help Silas."

Brody nodded at Lamar, and the other man unlocked the door. They hurried inside and Brody locked up behind them. He couldn't believe the bastards had tried to kill them doing a drive-by.

Caitlyn clung to Lamar for a few seconds then threw herself at him. He caught her and wrapped his arms around her in a fierce hug. She finally pulled back and rubbed her face with both hands.

"I'm going to go make coffee. I think we could all use some." She walked back toward the office where they had a small kitchenette.

"That was too fucking close, Brody. We could have easily been killed. I don't know what I would have done if I'd lost either of you." Lamar thrust his hands in his pockets.

"I feel the same way. I hope this is the end of it. I don't want to be watching our backs for the rest of our lives. How can we convince Caitlyn to stay with us if we might get her killed?"

"If this isn't the end, I don't want her staying here. I want her as far away from us as possible. I couldn't live knowing we had gotten her killed."

Brody nodded even as he felt his heart breaking at the thought of sending her away. It didn't matter. Her life was more important than his heart. In the meantime, they would wait for someone to come and tell them what was going on.

Several minutes later, Caitlyn returned with three mugs of steaming coffee. She handed one to each of them and cradled the last one between her hands. The dark liquid sloshed in the cup, betraying the soft tremors wracking her body. Brody gritted his teeth to keep from cursing. Instead, he set down his mug and pulled her back against him, wrapping his arms around her. He hoped to give her some of his strength.

She relaxed into his arms, and the little earthquakes slowly calmed. She sipped her coffee and laid her head back against his shoulder. Brody felt a moment's relief that she was in his arms and trusting him to keep her safe. Then reality took over and he slowly stood her up away from him.

"I want you to stay in the office until we find out what is going on. I don't want to take any chances that something else could happen. You should be out of the line of fire in there."

She turned around to glare at him. "I'm not a coward. I want to know what's going on. They were shooting at all of us, not just the two of you."

"I don't want anything to happen to you, Caitlyn. I can't concentrate on what needs to be done if I'm worried about you. Please don't argue with me on this." He squeezed her shoulders, keeping her close to him as they spoke.

He was aware of Lamar standing only feet away watching them. His brother would be making sure he wasn't stepping out of line. He wasn't. Brody knew he was right and she needed to be out of sight.

"I think you're being overprotective of me now. They have the men in custody. They aren't going to suddenly get loose and attack me again." She held up her hand when he started to contradict her. "But I'll stay in the office so you won't be dividing your attention while the deputies are here."

Brody felt his blood began to pump through his veins again. He pulled her into his arms and hugged her, coffee and all. Looking over to where Lamar was, he saw a look of relief flow across his brother's face.

"Okay. Get back to the office and stay there until one of us comes to get you. There should be plenty in there to keep you busy. It's where we start the paperwork for the bookkeeping anyway."

"Yeah, I noticed that the other day when I was here. I didn't want to fiddle around without your knowledge." Caitlyn turned and walked toward the office across the building.

Brody watched her until she disappeared inside. Then he turned back toward Lamar and grimaced. His brother looked as worried as he felt. What was taking the deputies so fucking long?

An urgent knock at the shop door jarred both men from their individual thoughts. Lamar was closest and stood to one side to answer it.

"Who is it?"

"It's Jace Vincent, Lamar."

Lamar unlocked the door and slowly opened the door. The deputy walked in and closed the door behind him.

"What's going on?" Brody demanded.

"We've got three men cuffed in the back of our vehicle. After running their names, it seems that not only do we have two guys with long rap sheets and a few warrants against them, but we have the president of Azzali Steele as well. Makes me wonder why the president of the company would be mixed up with drive-by shootings. Not only were they lousy shots, thank God, but they didn't have the sense to check their getaway route ahead of time."

"Talk about your stupidest criminals," Lamar said.

"Right. We're taking them down to the station for questioning. You guys should be fine now, but we'll let you know what we find out. Sheriff Tidwell is already there waiting on us."

"Thanks for the help, Jace."

"Glad we were driving by. Talk to you later." The deputy turned and walked out the door, closing it behind him.

Lamar locked it and turned to face Brody. "What do you think?"

"Tidwell said they were in league with the mob. There could be retaliation."

"Maybe. Do we send her away or keep her close?"

"Let's see what Tidwell comes up with. I've always trusted his instincts before."

Lamar nodded and they headed toward the office where Caitlyn was waiting for them. Brody needed to see her again to reassure himself that she hadn't been hurt. They'd been damn lucky.

He knocked on the office door and called out. "Caity, it's us. Unlock the door, baby."

The sound of the lock clicking let him know she had heard him. Then the door opened, and she stuck her head out with a giant smile aimed for them.

"What happened? Is it over?"

"They are headed to jail, but we don't know if there is anything else to worry about yet. The sheriff will talk to them and then let us know what he finds out. Until then, you've got to stay close to us and keep your head down."

"I can do that." She hugged them both then sat back at the desk. "I've got plenty to keep me busy here. Your files here aren't in much better shape than the ones you had at home."

Brody winced. He knew they weren't bookkeepers. They were machinists. Neither one of them had even taken bookkeeping or accounting or whatever the hell they called it now.

"Don't go getting defensive. Very few business owners keep their own books. Those that do probably shouldn't be."

"I don't know what we are going to do to keep them in line if you leave. They'll just get back in the same shape they were before you straightened them out."

"I'll help you figure them out. Maybe when I work on Brian's I can work on yours some, too."

"We better get to work, Brody. We've got a lot to get done today, including the online store business."

Brody sighed. Lamar was right. They needed to get to work. He was having a hard time leaving her, though. He wanted to stick around and just watch her work. Standing up, he winked at her and turned toward the door. Lamar already had it open and was walking through it. He followed behind his little brother, closing the door behind him. He heard the soft click of the lock even as his heart skipped a beat at the finality of the sound.

* * * *

Caitlyn pored over the paperwork stacked in piles on the desk. She had to work at concentrating on the numbers. Her head was still outside where they'd been shot at. She could almost hear the bullets popping the outside of the building around her head. Nothing like that had ever happened to her before. It made her screwed-up life with Harold seem small and insignificant. Maybe it was. Maybe she had needed this to put things in perspective. Was she putting more importance on the situation than it deserved?

She looked out the glass window at the men as they worked on something that looked a little like an engine. She couldn't help but admire their muscles as they glistened with sweat in the overhead lights. Each flex of muscle sent another bead of sweat down their brows or across their shoulders. Caitlyn wanted to follow where it rolled with her tongue.

She tore her eyes from the men and concentrated on the books once more. She had plenty of things to keep her busy. She didn't need to be making goo-goo eyes at Brody and Lamar while they were working. She couldn't fight her attraction to them, neither could she deny that she loved them, but could she live with them? Could she embrace the lifestyle that living with them would require?

She let it turn circles in her head while she concentrated on putting their business in order. Maybe later she would have an answer to that question. For now, she had work to do.

Sometime later, a knock at the door startled her into throwing her pen across the desk. She looked up into the amused eyes of Lamar standing at the door. She frowned at him before unlocking the door and finding her pen on the floor in front of the desk.

"Sorry. I didn't mean to scare you. I guess I thought you would see me walking across the floor."

"I'm really concentrating on the books. I guess I wasn't paying any attention to anything out there."

"Somehow I think I should be offended by that." Lamar kissed her on the forehead before grabbing two bottles of water from the fridge. "We needed some water. How are you doing?"

"I'm fine. How much longer till you're ready to head over to the store?"

"Brody wants to finish this project we're working on first. Shouldn't take more than another hour."

"Sounds good. I'm close to being finished with what I'm working on here. I'll need to work on it some more next week though."

Lamar nodded and winked as he walked out the door. She closed it and locked it behind him. Then she watched as he crossed the floor toward Brody, handing him a bottle of water once he reached him. Brody looked over toward her and saluted her with it. She waved and smiled then returned to working on their books.

An hour later, both men stood outside the door waiting on her to answer their knock. She smiled and unlocked the door. They were both soaking wet with sweat.

"Ready to head over to the store to finish up there?" Brody held the door open.

Caitlyn nodded and grabbed her purse. Then she waved them out ahead of her. She slipped past them and waited while Brody locked the office up. It didn't take them long to close the building down and drive over to Brian's store. Brody insisted that she remain in the locked truck until they had checked out the building to be sure it was safe.

Once inside, they quickly set up an assembly-line of packaging and labeling the items to be shipped. They had just loaded them into the truck to take them to the post office when Brody's cell rang.

"It's Tidwell. He's probably found out something by now."

Brody answered the phone and listened for a while before agreeing to meet them at the sheriff's office in thirty minutes. He hung up and filled them in.

"He said that we shouldn't have any further trouble but that he would explain everything once we got there. Let's mail these and head over there."

Caitlyn let the guys handle mailing the boxes. She sat in the truck, thinking about their close call and how everything could be okay so quickly when the mafia was involved. She still didn't feel totally safe right then.

It wasn't until they were sitting in the sheriff's office that she began to lose some of the worry she'd gathered up after being attacked earlier in the week. She'd believed that Brody and Lamar would have done everything in their power to keep her safe, but she knew they were two men. They hadn't even been armed that she was aware of. Now, she was surrounded by armed men.

Sheriff Tidwell walked into the room that was probably their conference room. She, Brody, Lamar, Deputy Vincent, and his partner Silas Atkins were all present at the table. The sheriff took the last seat at the head of the table and began talking.

"Tomas Azzali is the president of Azzali Steele of San Antonio. He is a small company branch out of Philadelphia. He's a second or third cousin to the big boss of Azzali. It seems that the big boss wasn't aware that Tomas was trying to build a mini-empire out here in Texas and isn't very happy with his cousin at the moment."

"So even though he has ties to the mafia, he isn't really part of them." Lamar leaned back in his chair.

"Right. He is probably part of their legit business practices that is supposed to keep the heat off of them back east. This has compromised their plans. I'm sure that Tomas will be dealt with severely. Once he gets out of prison here for attempted murder and aggravated assault."

"So the big boss isn't going to try and take over the business here." Brody didn't seem as convinced as Tidwell appeared to be.

Caitlyn could understand. He'd had his livelihood threatened and been shot at. She wasn't as convinced either.

"No. He's assured us that he has no intention of widening his business in this direction. He just wants to continue the local business that he'd started out working in San Antonio. He says he isn't greedy."

"Do you believe him?" Brody finally asked. "Because this is our business, not to mention our lives, on the line here."

"I believe him. He seems to be having a busy time out there right now as it is. He doesn't have the time or the manpower to spread himself thin right now. You can forget about Azzali Steele."

Caitlyn watched as Brody relaxed in his chair. He nodded and turned to Lamar. They exchanged a long look, and then he turned to look at her.

"How do you feel about it, Caity?"

"I trust the sheriff. I think everything is fine now."

"As long as you feel safe then I'll be happy. I don't want you to feel like you have to look over your shoulder all the time."

"I'm ready to go, Brody. Can we go back to your place now?" She suddenly felt tired and realized the adrenaline she'd been running on since the drive-by was beginning to fade.

"I agree with that." Lamar took her hand and pulled her to her feet.

Everyone at the table stood up as she and Lamar did. Brody took her other hand and they left the conference room together. She couldn't wait to get back to their place. She'd almost said *home* back there, and that worried her. She didn't need to be thinking about their house as home. She wasn't staying past next week. Was she?

Chapter Twenty

"Dinner was good, Caitydid. Thanks for cooking." Brody kissed her on the forehead as he walked by with his plate, heading toward the sink.

"I really enjoyed it. Meatloaf is my favorite." Lamar stood up with his plate and glass in his hand.

"I'm glad you both liked it. I enjoy cooking. I just don't like cooking for one, so I don't do it very often."

"You know if you stayed with us, you would be cooking for three." Lamar smiled at her.

Caitlyn wanted to say yes and stay with them, but she was afraid that it wouldn't work. What if a few months down the line they decided they didn't want to be tied down with her? Where would she be then? She would have a business there and have to start over again.

"What are you thinking about so hard over there, Caity?" Brody's expression said that he knew what she was thinking about. She hesitated, trying to figure out what to say.

"The truth. Don't avoid the question."

She put down the dishcloth and dried her hands. Turning toward where he and Lamar stood just inside the kitchen doorway, she licked her bottom lip and sighed.

"I'm just worried that you'll get tired of me and want out after a few months. I'm no one special. How can I possibly keep two men interested? I couldn't even keep one before."

"Are you comparing us to that scumbag?" Lamar demanded.

"No! I know you're nothing like him. I'm used to being on my own all the time. I don't know if I can change to fit into your lives. I don't want to wake up one day to find out that you are tired of me and then have to start over again."

She watched Brody walk around the table while rubbing his hands over his face. He stopped several steps in front of her.

"Caity, we want a chance to prove to you that we're in this for the long haul. You mean more to us than anything. Give us the chance to prove it. Now that we don't have to worry about someone coming at us from behind our backs, we can spend more time with you and show you how we feel."

"We have next week."

"What about the week after that? You said you were going to be here three weeks to make sure Tish knew how to handle the books." Lamar took a step forward, a serious expression on his face.

"I was thinking I would move back over there to work with them on their business."

"Stay with us instead. It would be like living with us and going to work every day. You can see how well it would all work for us." Lamar took another step toward her and was within touching distance now.

She glanced over at Brody and could tell that he had been expecting her to stay with them the entire time as well. She quickly searched back to figure out if she'd told them she would or not. She couldn't remember. It had all happened so quickly.

"But Brian…"

"Knows how we feel about you. We told him we wanted to court you. He'll expect you to stay with us if you're thinking about it. Give us a chance, Caitlyn." Brody stared down into her eyes as Lamar reached out and palmed her cheek.

How could she say no, especially when her heart was already theirs? She sighed and looked down at her feet. She couldn't. *God, leaving them was going to kill her.*

"Okay. I'll stay with you until I've made sure Tish is comfortable with the books. I'll make sure you're doing okay with yours, too."

Lamar grabbed her before Brody could and swung her around in his arms. Then he kissed her long and deep, wrapping her in his arms so that she couldn't move even if she wanted to.

"Lamar, carry her upstairs. I'm going to finish loading the dishwasher. I'll be up in a few minutes."

Lamar whooped for joy and picked her up in his arms. She clung to him as he climbed the stairs toward the bedroom. She expected him to let her down once they were in the room, but he continued to the bathroom and set her on the counter. He stood between her spread legs and nipped at her earlobe before licking his way down her neck to nip at the curve where it met her shoulder.

"What are you doing, Lamar?"

"Enjoying the taste of you. I'm making sure that I will always remember how you taste."

Before she could think of a reply to that, he claimed her mouth with his and plundered it with his teeth and tongue. She sighed and relaxed into his kiss. Then the sound of running water drew her from Lamar's hold.

She pulled back and looked over his shoulder to see Brody undressing next to the shower. He caught her eye and smiled as he unzipped his jeans and slowly pulled them down his hips. He wasn't wearing any underwear. His long, meaty cock stood out away from his body as he stood there. She couldn't take her eyes off of his body as he fisted his dick and pulled on it several times.

"Do you want some of that?" Lamar whispered into her ear.

"Please? I want you both." She pulled her eyes away from the sight of Brody's hand on his cock to plead with Lamar.

"First let's undress you and then we'll see."

She waited while he slowly pulled her T-shirt over her head. He made short work of her front-closure bra. Then he unfastened her jeans and had her lean back on her hands and lifted her hips so he could remove them. He took her panties at the same time.

"God, I love looking at your tits, Caity. They're perfect. I could suck on those big nipples of yours all day."

"Suck on them later, Lamar. The water is going to get cold," Brody interrupted him.

Lamar grinned and quickly kicked off his boots and jeans. He wasn't wearing underwear either. She took in his magnificent body as he helped her down from the counter and urged her toward the shower where Brody was waiting on them.

Caitlyn grabbed the soap from Brody and began soaping up a cloth and applied it to his body. She scrubbed him from shoulders to toes before turning and finishing Lamar's body as well. Then she had them rinse in the spray of the shower. She sank to her knees and took hold of their cocks in each of her hands.

"I'm going to suck you both off at the same time."

"Fuck, baby. You don't have to do that." Brody's voice was strained. She was sure it was because she had his cock in her hand.

"Be quiet, Brody, and hold on. I don't want either of you to fall in the process."

She leaned forward and licked Lamar's dick from balls to tip and then back down again. He closed his eyes but didn't make a sound. She shifted her attention to Brody and repeated the process. She watched his throat work as he swallowed when she ran the tip of her tongue around the mushroom cap of his cockhead.

"Does that feel good, Brody? Do you want more?"

"Fuck, yeah."

She smiled and lapped up the pearl of cum sitting in the slit on top of his cock. His quick hiss of breath made her smile. He was not quite as salty as Lamar was. His essence was a bit more tangy. She wrapped her mouth around his cockhead and sucked hard in hopes of another drop of the liquid.

She released him with a pop and turned to tease Lamar with her tongue. She licked up and down the stalk of his dick before reaching between his legs to caress his balls. He hissed out a quick breath before digging his hands in her hair. She moved over to Brody once more.

Over and over she sucked on them, never going very far down their cocks before changing to the other one. They cursed and massaged her scalp, but never once did they try to force her to suck them deeper. Her pussy was dripping wet now, and she wanted one of them inside of her. She stopped playing around and took first Lamar, then Brody to the back of her throat until they were close to erupting.

She squeezed their dicks with her throat muscles in an attempt to make them come, but neither one of them let go. Instead, they pulled her to her feet and wrapped her in their arms.

"You're next, Caity." Brody's raspy voice finally managed to get out despite the panting. "Not ready to come until we're inside of you."

Lamar rubbed his thick cock up and down the cleft of her ass cheeks before pulling away and stepping out of the now-cold shower. He reached back in and shut the water off. Then he grabbed a towel and held it open for her. She smiled and walked into it, letting him pat her dry.

Once they were all three dry, Brody prodded her toward the bed. He stopped her just short of climbing up.

"Lamar's going to get up first. I don't think either one of us can wait our turn to get inside of your hot body, so we're going to take you together."

"Yes!" She waited while Lamar rolled on a condom then quickly mounted his body to impale herself on his thick dick.

She was soaking wet, but her pussy put up a fight. It took them three tries before he was finally all the way inside her hot cunt. He wiggled, sending lightning shards of sensation through her body.

Then Brody was gently pushing her down to rest against Lamar's chest. He wrapped his arms around her to keep her in place. Even though she was prepared for what came next, she couldn't stop the soft gasp when something cold fell on her ass.

Brody spread her ass cheeks wide then slowly rubbed his thumb around her back hole, smearing more of the warming gel inside the opening of her ass. It had her pussy contracted around poor Lamar's dick.

"Easy, Caity. Don't make me come before we get to play."

"I can't help it. He touches me there and I shiver all over."

"You like for Brody to play with your ass, don't you, Caity."

"It feels so wrong."

Then Brody was adding more lube and pressing his finger inward, slowly popping through the resistant ring. She moaned and bit Lamar's shoulder. He grunted but didn't say anything. Instead, he began to rub her back in slow circles to help relax her.

More cold lube dropped on her ass, and a second finger began pressing forward in an effort to join the first one. She pushed out in an effort to relax her sphincter for him to get through. Once he had, she stilled and tried to relax against the fullness of the two fingers deep in her ass.

"Your ass is squeezing my fingers, baby. I can't wait to get inside and feel that squeeze on my cock. It's going to be pure heaven." Brody leaned over to whisper in her ear as he pumped the two fingers in and out of her ass.

"Please, Brody. Hurry. I need you inside of me."

Brody groaned and slowly pulled his fingers free of her tight hole. She felt him pressing against her dark rosette and prepared herself for the burn she knew was coming next. As his cock slowly pushed inside of her against the tight resistant ring, she pushed out and breathed through the dark burn until he finally popped through. He surged forward then stopped and let her adjust to his presence.

"Fuck, you're so damn tight."

Brody pulled part of the way out and tunneled forward once again until he was fully seated deep in her ass. She hissed out a breath and dug her nails into Lamar's shoulders. The pinch and burn slowly lessened as an itch took their places. She needed them to move now. The pressure of both of them inside her was beginning to get to her.

"Move, Brody. I need you to fuck me. Now!"

He grunted and pulled out as Lamar pressed upward, farther inside of her. Then he was pulling back and Brody thrust deep inside of her. They worked in tandem, rocking her between them. She moaned as it began to move together to send shards of excitement through her system. Her blood thickened into molten lava, surging through her veins and arteries until every cell in her body was alive with the fire that would soon consume her.

"She's sucking my dick so hard I'm not going to last, Brody." Lamar's strained voice seemed to be squeezed from him.

"Her fucking ass is like a vise grip without the teeth. I swear she's squeezing me on purpose."

Caitlyn couldn't have controlled her body enough to do any of it if her life had depended on it. She was as much at the mercy of the sensations as they were. No amount of holding back could stop what was coming. Pressure built inside her body, inside her head. It was going to kill her. There was no way she could live through the coming storm. It moved through her body despite her attempts at stopping it.

"God, Brody, Lamar. It's too much. Please, you've got to stop."

"Caity, it's going to be beautiful. Relax and go with it. Don't fight it, baby." Brody's voice sounded tight and far away.

She tried to say no again, but her throat was clogged with need. She needed this. Caitlyn knew that it would either kill her or remake her. She stopped fighting and sensations of pleasure began bombarding her from all directions. She felt her cunt tighten rhythmically around Lamar's cock as he moved in and out of her. Her ass sucked at Brody as he tunneled in and out of it. Both men groaned as she embraced her body's pleasures.

Just as she began to explode inside, she felt the men explode as well, filling their condoms with hot cum. It burned despite being contained inside the latex barriers. She felt it and knew they were satisfied. She relaxed past another barrier and embraced the explosion that sent her into a zone where she'd never been before. Every cell in her body contracted and relaxed over and over until her ears were ringing and her sight dimmed.

"Caitlyn? Baby, can you hear me?" Brody's voice sounded far away. Then Lamar's penetrated her foggy brain. "Are you asleep, baby?"

She couldn't answer them. The intense pleasure had drained her of everything. She had nothing left to use as energy. All she could do was hum her appreciation and pleasure. She hoped they would get it. She wasn't sure when she would be able to talk again. That orgasm had drained everything out of her, from her cum to her brain cells.

Somehow she figured they would turn it around to be all their doing. And she guessed it was in a way. She supposed she would just have to accept their smug expressions when she was able to see again. Right now, opening her eyes was too much trouble. Breathing seemed like too much trouble, but somehow her body was managing it. She could only be grateful.

Chapter Twenty-One

Lamar opened his eyes to the sight of Caitlyn's glorious hair mere inches from his face. He inhaled and smiled. She smelled like mint. He recognized the shampoo that had taken up residence in the bathroom. Pain sliced through his chest at the thought of it not being there in two weeks. They had to figure out a way to convince her she belonged with them.

He leaned forward and placed a soft kiss against the back of her head and concentrated on the feel of her skin beneath his hand. He had one on her waist and the other hand was beneath her head, under the pillow. She was wrapped around Brody like a mini octopus, its tentacles latched on in a death grip. Lamar had no doubt Brody was awake over there, enjoying the feel of her body against his. He had awakened just like that a time or two himself. It was pure heaven.

He wanted to wake her up with kisses and caresses but figured she needed more sleep. Instead, he carefully extracted himself and slipped out of bed. On his way to the bathroom, Brody called out in a quiet voice.

"Check the doors again when you get down and check for messages, too."

"Got it. Want me to wake you up anytime in particular?"

"Before lunch. I figure she needs the sleep."

"I'll fix sandwiches for us. You'll be hungry by then."

"Tell me about it."

Lamar chuckled at Brody's obvious need for breakfast. That was what he got for allowing them to play too long before passing out. Of course Caitlyn had passed out first. She'd been the smart one.

He quickly finished in the bathroom and dressed before slipping back into the bedroom and heading for the door. He avoided looking toward the bed in hopes that out of sight would mean out of mind, but that didn't work. He had to negotiate the stairs with thoughts of Caitlyn in the bed, naked and willing. It was a long walk down the stairs and into the kitchen alone in the dark. He flipped on the kitchen lights and waited while his eyes adjusted to the sudden light.

A quick glimpse through the window assured him that it was still early morning. A light fog covered the street about a hundred yards down the road on either side of them. He checked the doors and found them all locked with nothing out of place. Then he put on the coffee and waited for it to brew. With any luck, the scent of fresh coffee brewing would wake Caity up. He hoped she didn't startle awake and unman poor Brody in the process. He was lying on his back when Lamar had come downstairs.

He scrounged up more bread. It was fairly fresh, so he planned to make roast beef sandwiches out of the leftover beef from the day before. He pulled several blocks of wonderful flavorful cheese from the fridge.

His cell rang. He checked the number but didn't recognize it at first. When he answered, a strange voice replied. It was the owner of Azzali Steele and said that a meeting had been set up for three that afternoon with the three of them. They would meet at the diner. It would prove to be the easiest chore of the day. In the meantime, he needed to go pay the bills and run by the grocery store.

Lamar waited until nearly noon before hauling two cups of coffee upstairs to the bedroom. He set one on the bedside table and waved the coffee under their noses. Caity's wrinkled up, but Brody's eyes opened immediately. He sniffed and closed his eyes with a look of concentration there.

"I'll take care of the coffee. Help me get her up," Brody said in a muffled voice.

Lamar grinned and walked over to the bed. He pulled back the covers and exposed them to the cooler air in the room. Brody groaned but didn't fight it. Instead, he reached up with his free arm and tugged on Caitlyn's hair.

Lamar slowly counted to ten before getting serious about waking her up. They needed to dress, eat, and get to that meeting. He had a feeling it would be very important. The bigwig of Azzali Steele was in town from up northeast. He wanted to meet with them and discuss business. Lamar worried that once Brody found out he wouldn't want to go. Lamar had always had a more lenient attitude and thought the best of someone until proven otherwise.

"Lunch is ready, you two. Time to get up. We've got somewhere to be at three."

"Where?" Brody narrowed his eyes as he started rubbing on Caity's bare stomach.

"I'll tell you all about it as soon as we get downstairs to eat. It's nearly twelve and we have to be there by three."

"Fine." Brody glared at him but finished extracting himself from Caitlyn's hold. Then he rolled her over on her back and buried his face in her belly, blowing a raspberry until she squealed and sat up, pushing his head away.

"There, now. I'm going to dress. You can help her put on something to wear. Think you can manage that without ending up in bed with her?"

"Very funny, Brody. I've got her covered." He winced at how close to the truth his brother had pegged him. He would have to work hard not to slide in her pretty pussy right there and then.

"Caity, it's time to wake up. I've got lunch on the table waiting."

"Lunch? What happened to breakfast?" She buried her face in the pillow, muffling her voice.

Lamar pulled the pillow away from her. "Come on. We've got to be somewhere at three, babe. We need you to get up and dressed for us."

"Sure." She made a definite effort to sit up but failed miserably.

Lamar shook his head and pulled her upright by her shoulders. Then he pulled her to her feet using her arms. She stood there swaying on her feet but didn't collapse back to the bed like Lamar feared she would. He grabbed some clothes and helped her dress before he let he sit back down again. Then he helped her pull on socks and shoes.

"There, feel better now?"

She rolled her eyes at him. He guessed not. They walked down the stairs to the kitchen where he helped her up on a stool at the bar. She looked from him to the sandwich and back again. He had mercy on her and told her to go ahead and eat.

"Brody will be down soon enough."

He watched her take a bite into her sandwich with a sigh. She nodded as she chewed. Then Brody walked into the kitchen and lifted an eyebrow at her serious expression while she ate.

"Morning, man. What's up at three?"

"I got a phone call this morning from none other than the owner of Azzali Steele wanting to discuss the damage his cousin had started. So I figured we would be stupid not to see what he had to say."

"You're right. Where are we meeting him?"

"At the diner. It's a nice public place, and he is looking forward to a piece of the famous apple pie he's heard so much about. He plans to come unarmed and asks that we do the same."

"Fuck. More innocent blood around to watch out for."

I still think it's the best place."

Brody wiped a hand over his face. "You're right. It is. Well, the best thing we can do is follow his example and show up unarmed."

"Should we give the sheriff a heads-up on what is going on?" Lamar asked.

"That would probably be a good idea. He would be armed and have a reason to be."

"What's going on?" Caity had finished off her breakfast and was carrying her and Brady's plates to the sink.

"We're going to meet with the owner of Azzali Steele. He wants to talk about what his cousin tried to do. We want to see what his intentions are. If he plans to start something here, we need to nip that in the bud right now." Brody turned up his cup of coffee and drained it.

Lamar watched her face to see how she would react to that bit of news. When she didn't immediately start fussing about it, he took it as a sign she would be able to handle some of the more intense aspects of life in Riverbend. She needed a friend and confidant. Someone who could help her think through the different ways people lived in the small town.

"Why don't you hang around and talk with some of the women in the store next to Brian's place. It's a fetish wear shop. You'll probably enjoy browsing to see what all there is. I think they carry books there, too."

"Why can't I come with you two?"

"It could be dangerous, and we don't want you exposed if it is."

"I'll worry about you while you're gone."

Lamar hugged her and kissed her on the temple. "We've got it covered, baby. Just enjoy yourself and don't leave that store with anyone. Not even with someone you know."

She sighed and nodded. "All right, I'll stay there...for a while."

Lamar sighed as Brody ground his teeth.

"I'm not going to stay there all day. Hurry back."

They quickly cleaned up the kitchen then Lamar and Brody drove her to the fetish wear shop, Bits and Pieces. Lamar walked her inside and introduced her to Auria and Kathleen. He explained that they needed Caitlyn to stay with them for an hour or so.

"We'll be back as soon as we can. Find something fun to wear, Caity."

She rolled her eyes at him but let him kiss her on the cheek before he left.

Lamar hated the idea of leaving her anywhere without them to protect her, but he figured it was as good a place as any. He hurried back out to the truck and climbed in as Brody put it in gear.

When they pulled up at the diner, it was to find two other cars there besides the sheriff's car. One had out-of-state tags. The other had Texas tags that made them from the San Antonio area. Lamar drew in a deep breath and looked over at Brody.

"You ready?"

"Yep, let's get this over with and get our woman back before they turn her into a fetish queen."

They climbed out of the truck and walked into the diner. The sheriff was sitting close to the front door nursing a cup of coffee when they walked by. In the back of the room crammed into one booth were four guys. Three of them were obviously muscle. They wore T-shirts stretched tightly over their impressive physiques. The fourth man was easily in his sixties, maybe even early seventies. He looked like he tried to keep in shape, but age would only allow so much before the normal breakdown of tissues took its toll.

He and Brody nodded at the sheriff. Then they approached the group in the back with their hands out to their sides. Once they had gotten within eight feet of them, they stopped and waited for the old man to speak.

After what seemed like hours, the man patted his mouth with his napkin before dropping it into his plate. He pushed the plate aside and folded his hands on the tabletop. Then he just stared at them for a few minutes. The hired muscle stared around the room mostly, but they were finely attuned to their boss.

"We're here, what did you want to discuss?" Lamar had had enough of standing there staring at each other.

"First of all, I'm Ferdinando Azzali. My father started Azzali Steele nearly ninety-eight years ago. We've prided ourselves on being totally up-front and honest with our customers, and if I'm not, they will be the first to turn me in." He sat back in his chair.

"Enough of this." Brody didn't have the patience for this. "What did you want us for?"

"Why do I have to want you for anything? Maybe I just want to apologize for my family's obvious mistake in person. He is overly ambitious, not overly smart."

"Yeah, we got that from him right off." Lamar continued to watch the other men at the table.

"He will be dealt with once he is released from jail. I wish you had informed us before you involved the police. We would have handled it without their involvement, and all of this would have been over."

"Don't count on it. The law around here is very thorough. They would have traced down the connection and hassled your people anyway." Brody slipped his hands into his pockets.

Lamar considered doing the same thing because his hands were beginning to sweat.

"I suppose this is a small community where everyone knows everyone, so you are probably right. It wouldn't have been possible to keep it quiet." The older man sighed and waved his hand in the air as if to clear it of some strong smell. "I'm here for another reason as well."

"What would that be?" Brody asked.

"I would like to keep my business open in San Antonio. Can we agree not to push into each other's territory?"

"There's more than enough work for both of us in the area."

"We like to keep competition to a minimum. Keeps business flowing and prices reasonable for everyone."

"So you want to set up a territory of sorts. What's in it for us?"

"We promise not to invade your area and will be happy to help you with any other problems that crop up in your area."

Brody frowned at that. Lamar had a feeling the old man's idea of help would be a violent one. He planted his hands on his hips in an effort to dry them without being obvious.

"We have no intentions of spreading out into San Antonio. If you stay away from us and the general Austin area as well, we won't bother you. How would that work for you?"

The older man sat back in the booth and thought about it for several seconds. Then he nodded and held out his hand.

Brody walked up and shook the old man's hand, and Ferdinando pulled him down into a hug. Lamar wasn't too thrilled with the idea of hugging the guy, but he shook his hand anyway. The hug turned out to be quick and painless.

"We'll be on our way now." They filed out of the booth and walked past Brody and Lamar as they did.

Everyone, including the sheriff, walked outside and climbed into their vehicles. Lamar and Brody waited until the two Cadillacs disappeared from sight. Once they were gone, Lamar waited on Brody to decide what to do next. His brother stared around the area then climbed back up in the cab of the truck and waited on Lamar to buckle up before he turned them around to go back to the shop.

He was out of the truck almost before he had put it in park and heading toward the fetish shop. Lamar had no doubt he was totally into Caitlyn. He didn't want to be away from her any more than Lamar did.

Auria answered the back door and called over her shoulder to the others. "Come on in. We're just going over the basics of the different lifestyles around here. She's a sturdy sort, Lamar. You two could do better, but I can tell you've got your heart set on her."

"She belongs to us now." Brody wasn't going leave until Auria acknowledged that Caity was theirs.

"Agreed. She belongs to you."

At that moment, Caitlyn and Kathleen walked out of the front of the store. Caitlyn crossed to stand between him and Brody. She looked fine and didn't seem to be in the least stressed out. That was good. The women must not have gotten into too much detail about the area. She didn't seem spooked or nervous.

"Did you enjoy your visit?"

"I had a great time. I'm thinking that maybe the people here are pretty good. They're friendly, that's for sure." She chuckled and shook her head. "And lo and behold but they need help with their books, too. Did you know that when you dropped me off here?"

Lamar shook his head. "Nope. We've never talked finances before."

"Let's get back to the house." Brody edged them toward the back door of the fetish shop.

"Thanks, ladies, for keeping Caity company while we handled some business."

"Not a problem, Brody. She's welcome over here anytime." Kathleen waved them off and closed the door behind them.

"What did you girls talk about?" Lamar was interested in finding out. How she reacted to them and the gossip around town could be an important step toward keeping her as their wife or losing her.

"A little bit about a lot of things. Most of it seemed like gossip to me, though. I'm not much on gossip."

"What did you think about Auria and Kathleen?"

"Well, at first I thought they might be sexual partners, but they aren't. Then I had to figure out what their relationship was other than friends and business partners."

"Did you figure it out?"

"Yeah, Kathleen keeps Auria reined in. She is a bit wild and needs someone strong to keep her from getting into trouble and stuff."

"It's a unique relationship, that's for sure." Brody started the truck.

"Enough about that. I'm ready for a nap. I'm tired. I help them put up inventory. Some of that stuff is heavy."

Lamar laughed and pulled her close to him so he could kiss her. She kissed him back then licked across his bottom lip. Maybe she was wanting more than just a nap. Lamar was all over it. He could use a little activity himself. He watched her slip her hand down the front of Brody's shirt until she reached his groin. There she squeezed around where his cock and balls would be seated in his jeans on the truck seat. His swift intake of breath told him that Brody was as in as Lamar.

The minute Brody had the truck parked, Lamar and Caitlyn were unbuckled and climbing out of the truck. Brody cursed and hurried to unlock the garage door before they tore the door down trying to get in. He locked the truck and followed them inside. Lamar looked back to be sure that Brody was following them. He caught his brother's eye and grinned. Brody was following them and using the opportunity to stare at Caitlyn's sweet ass all the way up the stairs.

Chapter Twenty-Two

The week passed fast as they settled into a routine of sorts. They spent the majority of the day at the shop where they worked, stopping for lunch and either eating something they had brought or eating at the diner. They broke off from the shop around three thirty and worked on the online store until around six. Everything they had wrapped on one day got mailed out at lunch the next day. It was working pretty well.

Brian, Andy, and Tish were due back the next day. Caitlyn was both excited to see them and dreading it all at the same time. It meant that her days there were numbered in the single digits now. Once Tish proved to be proficient with the bookkeeping system for both the store and the online business, she wouldn't have a reason to stick around anymore. It would be time for her to leave.

Pain blossomed inside her chest as if she'd been shot. For a minute, she thought she would pass out from it. Then it slowly subsided and she felt an overwhelming emptiness begin to take its place. This was how she would feel once she left Riverbend and Brody and Lamar.

"Why the sad face, Caity?" Lamar pulled her into his arms and looked down at her.

"Nothing. How is the project coming?"

"Just finished it. We're thinking about going out for a celebration dinner tonight. Are you up for a steak and maybe some dancing?"

"Sounds good." She would take every possible opportunity to be close to them while she could.

They finished up at the store early and hurried through showers and dressing to make it to the steak house by seven. Dinner proved to be fun and light, but once they arrived at the bar, the guys got quiet and kept their hands on some part of her body at all times. She could tell they were beginning to think along the same lines she was. This was the beginning of the end. She shook it off. She didn't want to think about that tonight. She wanted to have fun tonight.

"Okay, who's dancing with me first?" She stood up and set her beer on the table.

Lamar stood up and pulled her up tight against him.

"I've got you, Caity." He pulled her along behind him as they headed toward the dance floor.

She looked back to see Brody watching them with a quiet expression on his face. She didn't know what to make of that. Brody might brood or be angry, but he didn't look quiet. She frowned but soon changed her expression when Lamar wrapped his arms around her while they danced.

He was a great dancer, and they stayed out on the floor through two more songs. Finally, she managed to get him to take her back to the table to rest.

"I'm obviously not in as good a shape as you are. Have mercy on me."

He chuckled and helped her sit down before he sat next to her.

"Did he wear you out already?" Brody looked amused as he shook his head.

"I'm not used to doing anything other than sit in front of a computer all day."

"That's why there are weekends, so you can get out and exercise some." Lamar squeezed her thigh.

"Speaking of exercise," Brody began. "I'm looking forward to tonight. I bet your panties are wet already after all that rubbing around you did with Lamar a while ago."

"You're terrible." She couldn't help the blush that warmed her face.

They both laughed and leaned in on either side of her to nibble and lick her neck. She laid a hand on each of their chests and tried without real conviction to push them away. Neither man budged. She was sure by the time they finished that her neck was a solid line of red skin on both sides. She should be so embarrassed, but for some reason, it didn't bother her. Maybe it was because there were other threesomes there as well. She finally put a stop to their mauling by grabbing their cocks with her hands in their laps.

"Right here with you, babe. Whatever you want." Lamar's grin told her that they weren't taking her seriously.

"We'll take good care of you, Caitydid. Just tell us what you want." Brody actually pushed his dick farther into her hand.

"You guys are incorrigible. I can't get a hand up on you for anything."

"You love us like we are, though, right?" Lamar asked in a teasing voice.

"Yeah, I love you like you are." She froze. She hadn't meant to tell them.

Caitlyn glanced at them through lowered lashes and realized they hadn't taken her seriously. It was all in fun and games. She sighed and returned to their games. Between dancing, drinking, and screwing around, she was totally exhausted by the time Brody called it a night. They each took an arm and helped her out of the bar and down the road where they had parked the truck.

It took Lamar two tries to get her up in the cab of the truck. Brody was laughing so hard at them that he couldn't help them. Finally, they were all strapped in and ready to go. Lamar was busy trying to eat her breasts through her clothes while Brody negotiated the streets to get them home safely.

"You two need to calm down a bit over there. You're going to get us thrown in jail for indecent behavior." Brody's amused voice sounded far away as Lamar's hands pinched and prodded her nipples through her clothes.

"He's just jealous that he has to drive and can't play with you."

"I'm going to have my turn, but not if you get us thrown in jail," he reminded them.

Lamar pulled back and looked around. Then he shrugged and continued where he'd left off.

Caitlyn giggled and fought his lightning-fast hands. "Hold up, Lamar. We're almost home. Just a few more seconds and we'll be in the drive."

"Umm, home. I like the sound of that coming from your mouth."

Caitlyn froze. She'd said it without thinking about it, but Lamar had caught on to it. What did she do?

"Caity? What's wrong, babe?" Lamar pulled back to look down in her face.

"Nothing. I was just trying to get ready to get out. I've got to put my clothes back right before we get to the house."

She saw Lamar and Brody exchange glances. They had caught on that she'd changed her verbiage from *home* to *house*. What did they expect? She was supposed to leave any day now.

They all three climbed out of the truck in silence. Brody unlocked the door and stood aside for her to enter first. They headed for the kitchen, and when she pulled out a beer, the others followed suit.

"We need to talk about it, Caitlyn. They'll be home tomorrow." Brody's voice sounded brittle.

"I know. But I don't see what there is to talk about. I already told you that I would be leaving for Austin once they were back and Tish felt comfortable with the books."

"I guess we were thinking, um, hoping that you would change your mind. You seemed to be happy here. We all get along just fine," Lamar said.

"We do. It's not that. I'm scared that we'll get tired of each other after a while. You'll find someone you really want to be with and then I'll get left out in the cold again."

She stared at them standing there. They could have any woman they wanted with their gorgeous bodies. All she knew was that they were handsome men with devilish looks in their eyes, and she was so in love with them that it was pathetic.

"Baby, we're never going to get tired of you. You mean everything to us. We want you to be with us all the time." Brody looked as if he wanted to reach out to her.

Caitlyn wanted to believe him. She wanted to trust that everything he said was the truth so she could stay there in Riverbend. Part of her did believe him. It was the other part that kept her from saying yes. The part that was afraid of being hurt again.

She quickly dried her tears and turned around when Lamar walked up behind her. He pulled her into his embrace and told her how beautiful she looked and that he wanted to fuck her pretty pussy until she passed out.

"It wouldn't be the first time." She knew he was trying to take her mind off of everything.

"You weren't complaining at the time."

"I wasn't about to. That was the best sex ever." She had almost said loving ever and stopped herself in time.

"Sounds like a challenge to me. What about you?" Lamar turned to Brody.

"I think I'm up for a challenge." Brody pulled her into a toe-curling kiss that took her breath away.

"Oh, my God."

"My turn." Lamar gave her little time to recover before he was sucking on her tongue and massaging her scalp with his nails.

When he finally pulled back, she was too dizzy to stand up straight. Brody picked her up and carried her upstairs to the bedroom. If they made love to her now, she'd cave for sure. She needed fast and wild to keep her promise to herself not to change her mind about Austin. Unfortunately, neither man was cooperating. She slid down Brody's painfully aroused body. Once her feet touched the floor, she tried to turn and head in the opposite direction of the bed.

"No, you don't. We've got some things to settle tonight." Brody's voice sounded serious now instead of aroused.

"What things?"

Only moments before he had been ready to take her to bed. Now he sounded like all he wanted to do was talk. Confusion clouded her mind.

"You're moving in with us permanently sort of things."

"Brody, we've talked about it. I have to move to Austin."

"No, you don't. You have a perfectly good business opportunity here, and you admitted that you would rather work for yourself than someone else. You don't have to do anything if you don't want to, though. We can support you just fine, baby."

"I know you can, but I want to work. Besides, I have to in order to pay for my home." Caitlyn realized that she wasn't going to move to Austin after all. She had fallen in love with Riverbend and the people there. Everyone looked out for each other and were friendly. She took a deep breath and faced the two men.

"I've about decided to live here, Brody, but I can't live with you and Lamar. It would screw up our relationship and hurt yours with my brother and his family."

"How can it possibly hurt our relationship with your family?" Brody shook his head.

"Brian will always interfere with my life. You guys aren't going to handle that well."

"Things are different in Riverbend when it comes to families. Once you are our responsibility, Brian will back off."

Brody stared up at the ceiling as if it could provide the answers he needed.

She looked back at Brody and Lamar. She opened her mouth to explain, but nothing would come out. Caitlyn tried to come up with another reason she couldn't live with them and nothing would come to her. Even her old standbys of they'd find someone else they wanted more and they'd eventually get tired of her constant arguments weren't doing the trick. She wasn't working them out of her system either.

"Caitlyn, how do you know it won't work if you won't even give us a chance? We've been living together for nearly three weeks and done great. That alone should show you how well we fit together."

"I'm scared, Brody. What do I do if down the line one of you doesn't want me anymore? How am I supposed to deal with that?"

"It isn't going to happen, Caitydid. Nothing could ever come between the three of us." Brody seemed to want to say something more but held back.

Lamar poked him then stepped closer to her. "Caitlyn, I love you. I've loved you almost from the moment I laid eyes on you in that ditch. I can't stand the idea of your not living with us."

"Oh, Lamar. Are you sure it's me you love?"

"Yes, Caity. It's you. Only you."

She turned and looked up at Brody. The other man had a strained expression on his face and bunched muscles in his neck and shoulders.

"It's okay, Brody. You can tell me later whatever is on your mind. All of this is more than I can handle. I need to go to bed."

She started to get ready for bed and almost told them to leave her alone. She didn't want company, but it was their bedroom, and the truth was, she knew she couldn't sleep without them in bed with her.

Instead, she stripped down to her panties and climbed into bed without saying anything. They stripped as well and got in bed on either side of her. Neither man touched her as they lay there, each in their own thoughts.

Caitlyn wanted to tell them how she felt, tell them that she loved them more than life itself. She was afraid to. Frustration brought tears to her eyes once again. Did she really have to live somewhere else? Why couldn't she live with them?

Brody touched her first. He laid his big hand across her belly and scooted closer to her. She felt the first tear slide from her eyes. Then Lamar moved closer and wrapped his leg over hers, laying his hand just under her breast.

Lamar had said that he loved her and she believed him. She felt like Brody loved her as well, but he hadn't said the words. But then neither had she. How could she be sure of his feelings for her if he didn't say the words? They clashed against each other all the time. Without love, he would get tired of that—tired of her.

Everything kept circling in her head. Should she take a chance and live with them or play it safe and get her own place? Once they had been around her for a long time they might change their minds. If only Brody truly loved her.

"Caity?" Brody's deep voice pulled her from her thoughts.

"Yeah?"

"I love you, baby. I don't want you to go."

"We both love you more than anything in the world, Caity." Lamar spoke up from the other side of her.

"Give us a chance to show you how much we love you."

"I don't have to live with you for you to show me, Lamar."

"Move in with us, baby. Let us help take care of you. We'll give you anything you want that we can get."

"Oh, Brody. I already have what I want more than anything."

Lamar stiffened next to her. "What is that, Caity?"

"The two of you. I love you both so much it hurts to think of losing you."

The two men whooped out *hell, yes* and squeezed her within an inch of her life. She hugged them back and reveled in their kisses. She was making the right decision. She knew it in her heart.

"I'll move in with you under one condition."

"Anything." They spoke at the same time.

"I handle the books for your business from now on. I really don't want to have to straighten them out every year before tax season," she teased.

"Honey, you can handle anything you want if it means having you at home with us from now on." Brody kissed her and whispered in her ear some of the dirty things he wanted to do to her.

Caitlyn giggled and turned to Lamar for help. He shook his head and began nibbling along her jaw. Each of them began exploring her body with their hands making it nearly impossible to think.

She'd promised that when things settled down after the mafia incident she was going to count her blessings, and she finally had. Two of the biggest ones were lying on either side of her, and she'd almost walked away from them. Caitlyn said a prayer of thanks and then snuggled down between her two men as they pleasured her body. Her brother and his new family would be coming home in the morning and she was going to be living with the best things that had ever happened to her. She didn't think she could count any higher than that.

THE END

WWW.MARLAMONROE.COM

ABOUT THE AUTHOR

Marla Monroe lives in the southern part of the United States. She writes sexy romance from the heart and often puts a twist of suspense in her books. She is a nurse and works in a busy hospital but finds plenty of time to follow her two passions, reading and writing. You can find her in a bookstore or a library at any given time. Marla would love for you to visit her at her blog at themarlamonroe.blogspot.com and leave a comment. Or you can reach her by e-mail at themarlamonroe@yahoo.com.

For all titles by Marla Monroe, please visit
www.bookstrand.com/marla-monroe

Siren Publishing, Inc.
www.SirenPublishing.com

Lightning Source UK Ltd.
Milton Keynes UK
UKHW010719061118
331851UK00013B/1150/P